THE
BOY SCOUT
AVIATORS

GEORGE DURSTON

1st WORLD
LIBRARY
Literary Society

The Boy Scout Aviators

George Durston

© 1st World Library – Literary Society, 2005
PO Box 2211
Fairfield, IA 52556
www.1stworldlibrary.org
First Edition

LCCN: 2005906476

Softcover ISBN: 1-4218-1532-X
Hardcover ISBN: 1-4218-1432-3
eBook ISBN: 1-4218-1632-6

Purchase *"The Boy Scout Aviators"*
as a traditional bound book at:
www.1stWorldLibrary.org/purchase.asp?ISBN=1-4218-1532-X

1st World Library Literary Society is a nonprofit
organization dedicated to promoting literacy by:

- Creating a free internet library accessible from any
computer worldwide.
- Hosting writing competitions and offering book
publishing scholarships.

The Boy Scout Aviators
contributed by Tim, Ed & Rodney
in support of
1st World Library Literary Society

CHAPTER I

SERIOUS NEWS

"As long as I can't be at home," said Harry Fleming, "I'd rather be here than anywhere in the world I can think of!"

"Rather!" said his companion, Dick Mercer. "I say, Harry, it must be funny to be an American!"

Harry laughed heartily.

"I'd be angry, Dick," he said, finally, "if that wasn't so English - and so funny! Still, I suppose that's one reason you Britishers are as big an empire as you are. You think it's sort of funny and a bit of a misfortune, don't you, to be anything but English ?"

"Oh, I say, I didn't quite mean that," said Dick, flushing a little. "And of course you Americans aren't just like foreigners. You speak the same language we do - though you do say some funny things now and then, old chap. You know, I was ever so surprised when you came to Mr. Grenfel and he let you in our troop right away!"

"Didn't you even know we had Boy Scouts in America?" asked Harry. "My word as you English would say. That is the limit! Why, it's spread all over the country with us. But of course we all know that it started here - that Baden-Powell thought of the idea!"

"Rather!" said Dick, enthusiastically. "Good old Bathing-Towel! That's what they used to call him at school, you know, before he ever went into the army at all. And it stuck to him, they say, right through. Even after Mafeking he was called that. Now, of course, he's a lieutenant general, and all sorts of a swell. He and Kitchener and French are so big they don't get called nicknames much more."

"Well, I'll tell you what I think," said Harry, soberly. "I think he did a bigger thing for England when he started the Boy Scout movement than when he defended Mafeking against the Boers!"

"Why, how can you make that out?" asked Dick, puzzled. "The defence of Mafeking had a whole lot to do with our winning that war!"

"That's all right, too," said Harry. "But you know you may be in a bigger war yet than that Boer War ever thought of being."

"How can a war think, you chump?" asked the literal-minded Dick.

Again Harry roared at him.

"That's just one of our funny American ways of saying things, Dick," he explained. "I didn't mean that, of course. But what I do mean is that every-one over here in Europe seems to think that there will be a big war sometime - a bigger war than the world's ever seen yet."

"Oh, yes!" Dick nodded his understanding, and grew more serious. "My pater - he's a V. C., you know - says that, too. He says we'll have to fight Germany, sooner or later. And he seems to think the sooner the better, too, before they get too big and strong for us to have an easy time with them."

"They're too big now for any nation to have an easy time with them," said Harry. "But you see what I mean now, don't you,

George Durston

Dick? We Boy Scouts aren't soldiers in any way. But we do learn to do the things a soldier has to do, don't we?"

"Yes, that's true," said Dick. "But we aren't supposed to think of that."

"Of course not, and it's right, too," agreed Harry. "But we learn to be obedient. We learn discipline. And we get to understand camp life, and the open air, and all the things a soldier has to know about, sooner or later. Suppose you were organizing a regiment. Which would you rather have - a thousand men who were brave and willing, but had never camped out, or a thousand who had been Boy Scouts and knew about half the things soldiers have to learn? Which thousand men would be ready to go to the front first?"

"I never thought of that!" said Dick, mightily impressed. "But you're right, Harry. The Boy Scouts wouldn't go to war themselves, but the fellows who were grown up and in business and had been Boy Scouts would be a lot readier than the others, wouldn't they? I suppose that's why so many of our chaps join the Territorials when they are through school and start in business?"

"Of course it is! You've got the idea I'm driving at, Dick. And you can depend on it that General Baden-Powell had that in his mind's eye all the time, too. He doesn't want us to be military and aggressive, but he does want the Empire to have a lot of fellows on call who are hard and fit, so that they can defend themselves and the country. You see, in America, and here in Enland, too, we're not like the countries on the Continent. We don't make soldiers of every man in the country."

"No - by Jove, tey do that, don't they, Harry? I've got a, cousin who's French. And he expects to serve his term in the army. He's in the class of 1918. You see, he knows already when he will have to go, and just where he will report - almost the regiment he'll join. But he's hoping they'll let him be in the cavalry, instead of the infantry or the artillery."

"There you are! Here and in America, we don't have to have such tremendous armies, because we haven't got countries that we may have to fight across the street - you know what I mean. England has to have a tremendous navy, but that makes it unnecessary for her to have such a big army."

"I see you've got the idea exactly, Fleming," said a new voice, breaking into the conversation. The two scouts looked up to see the smiling face of their scoutmaster, John Grenfel. He was a big, bronzed Englishman, sturdy and typical of the fine class to which he belonged - public school and university man, first-class cricketer and a football international who had helped to win many a hard fought game for England from Wales or Scotland or Ireland. The scouts were returning from a picnic on Wimbledon Common, in the suburbs of London, and Grenfel was following his usual custom of dropping into step now with one group, now with another. He favored the idea of splitting up into groups of two or three on the homeward way, because it was his idea that one of the great functions of the Scout movement was to foster enduring friendships among the boys. He liked to know, without listening or trying to overhear, what the boys talked about; often he would give a directing word or two, that, without his purpose becoming apparent, shaped the ideas of the boys.

"Yes," he repeated. "You understand what we're trying to do in this country, Fleming. We don't want to fight - we pray to God that we shall never have to. But, if we are attacked, or if the necessity arises, we'll be ready, as we have been ready before. We want peace - we want it so much and so earnestly that we'll fight for it if we must."

Neither of the boys laughed at what sounded like a paradox. His voice was too earnest.

"Do you think England is likely to have to go to war soon - within a year or so, sir?" asked Harry.

"I pray not," said Grenfel. "But we don't know, Fleming. For the last few years - ever since the trouble in the Balkans finally flamed up - Europe has been on the brink of a volcano. We don't know what the next day may bring forth. I've been afraid -" He stopped, suddenly, and seemed to consider.

"There is danger now," he said, gravely. "Since the Archduke Franz Ferdinand of Austria was assassinated, Austria has been in an ugly mood. She has tried to blame Servia. I don't think Russia will let her crush Servia - not a second time. And if Russia and Austria fight there is no telling how it may spread."

"You'd want us to win, wouldn't you, Harry, if we fought?" asked Dick, when Mr. Grenfel had passed on to speak to some of the others.

"Yes, I think I would - I know I would, Dick," said Harry, gravely. "But I wouldn't want to see a war, just the same. It's a terrible thing."

"On, it wouldn't last long," said Dick, confidently. "We'd lick them in no time at all. Don't you think so?"

"I don't know - I hope so. But you can't ever be sure."

"I wonder if they'd let us fight?"

"No, I don't think they would, Dick. There'd be plenty for the Boy Scouts to do though, I believe."

"Would you stay over here if there was a war, Harry? Or would you go home?"

"I think we'd have to stay over here, Dick. You see, my father is here on business, not just for pleasure. His company sent him over here, and it was understood he'd stay several years. I don't think the war could make any difference."

"That's why you're here, then, is it? I used to wonder why you went to school over here instead of in America."

"Yes. My father and mother didn't want me to be so far from them. So they brought me along. I was awfully sorry at first, but now it doesn't seem so bad."

"I should think not!" said Dick, indignantly. "I should think anyone would be mighty glad of a chance to come to school over here instead of in America! Why, you don't even play cricket over there, I've been told!"

"No, but we play baseball," said Harry, his eyes shining. "I really think I miss that more than anything else here in England. Cricket's all right - if you can't play baseball. It's a good enough game."

"You can play," admitted Dick, rather grudgingly. "When you bowl, you've got some queer way of making the ball seem to bend -"

"I put a curve on it, that's all!" said Harry, with a laugh. "If you'd ever played baseball, you'd understand that easily enough. See? You hold the ball like this - so that your fingers give it a spin as it leaves your hand."

And he demonstrated for his English friend's benefit the way the ball is held to produce an out-curve.

"Your bowlers here don't seem to do that - though they do make the ball break after it hits the ground. But the way I manage it, you see, is to throw a ball that doesn't hit the ground in front of the bat at all, but curves in. If you don't hit at it, it will hit the stumps and bowl you out; if you do hit, you're likely to send it straight up in the air, so that some fielder can catch it."

"I see," said Dick. "Well, I suppose it's all right, but it doesn't seem quite fair."

Harry laughed, but didn't try to explain the point further. He liked Dick immensely; Dick was the first friend he had made in England, and the best, so far. It was Dick who had tried to get him to join the Boy Scouts, and who had been immensely surprised to find that Harry was already a scout. Harry, indeed, had done two years of scouting in America; he had been one of the first members of a troop in his home town, and had won a number of merit badges. He was a first-class scout, and, had he stayed with his troop, would certainly have become a patrol leader. So he had had no trouble in getting admission to the patrol to which Dick belonged.

It had been hard for Harry, when his father's business called him to England, to give up a all the friendships and associations of his boyhood. Had been hard to leave school; to tear up, by the roots, all the things that bound him to his home. But as a scout he had learned to be loyal and obedient. His parents had talked things over with him very frankly. They had understood just how hard it would be for him to go with them. But his father had made him see how necessary it was.

"I want you to be near your mother and myself just now, especially, Harry," he had said. "I want you to grow up where I can see you. And, more-over, it won't hurt you a bit to know something about other countries. You'll have a new idea of America when you have seen other lands, and I believe you'll be a better American for it. You'll learn that other countries have their virtues, and that we can learn some things from them. But I believe you'll learn, too, to love America better than ever. When we go home you'll be broader and better for your experience."

And Harry was finding out that his father had been right. At first he had to put up with a good deal. He found that the English boys he met in school felt themselves a little superior. They didn't look down on him, exactly, but they were, perhaps the least bit sorry for him because he was not an Englishman, always a real misfortune in their sight.

He had resented that at first. But his Boy Scout training stood him in good stead. He kept his temper, and it was not long before he began to make friends. He excelled at games; even the English games that were new and strange to him presented few difficulties to him. As he had explained to Dick, cricket was easy for any boy who could play baseball fairly well. And it was the same way with football. After the far more strenuous American game, he shone at the milder English football, the Rugby game, which is the direct ancestor of the sport in America.

All these things helped to make Harry popular. He was now nearly sixteen, tall and strong for his age, thanks to the outdoor life he had always lived. An only son, he and his father had always been good friends. Without being in any way a molly-coddle, still he had been kept safe from a good many of the temptations that beset some boys by the constant association with his father. It was no wonder, therefore, that John Grenfel, as soon as he had talked with Harry and learned of the credentials he bore from his home troop, had welcomed him enthusiastically as a recruit to his own troop.

It had been necessary to modify certain rules. Harry, of course, could not subscribe to quite the same scout oath that bound his English fellows. But he had taken his scout oath as a tenderfoot at home, and Grenfel had no doubts about him. He was the sort of boy the organization wanted, whether in England or America, and that was enough for Grenfel.

Though the boys, as they walked toward their homes, did not quite realize it, they were living in days that were big with fate. Far away, in the chancelleries of Europe, and, not so far away, in the big government buildings in the West End of London, the statesmen were even then making their best effort to avert war. No one in England, perhaps, really believed that war was coming. There had been war scares before. But the peace of Europe had been preserved for forty years or more, through one crisis after another. And so it was a stunning surprise, even to Grenfel, when, as they came into Putney High street, just before they reached Putney Bridge, they met a swam of newsboys excitedly shrieking extras.

"Germany threatens Russia!" they yelled. "War sure!"

Mr. Grenfel brought a paper, and the scouts gathered about him while he read the news that was contained on the front page, still damp from the press.

"I'm afraid it's true," he said, soberly. "The German Emperor has threatened to go to war with Russia, unless the Czar stops mobilizing his troops at once. We shall know tonight. But I think it means war! God save England may still keep out of it!"

For that night a meeting at Mr. Grenfel's home in West Kensington had long been planned. He lived not far from the street in which both Harry and Dick lived. And, as the party broke up, on the other side of Putney Bridge, Dick, voicing the general feeling, asked a question.

"Are we to come tonight, sir?" he said. "With this news - ?"

"Yes - yes, indeed," said the scoutmaster. "If war is to come, there is all the more reason for us to be together. England may need all of us yet."

Dick had asked the question because, like all the others, he felt something that was in the air. He was sobered by the news, although, like the rest, he did not yet fully understand it. But they all felt that there had been a change. As they looked about at the familiar sight about them they wondered if, a year from then, everything would still be the same. War? What did it mean to them, to England?

"I wonder if my father will go to war!" Dick broke out suddenly, as he and Harry walked along.

"I hadn't thought of that!" said Harry, startled. "Oh, Dick, I'm sorry! Still, I suppose he'll go, if his country needs him!"

CHAPTER II

QUICK WORK

At home, Harry had an early dinner with his father and mother, who were going to the theatre. They lived in a comfortable house, which Mr. Fleming had taken on a five-year lease when they came to England to live. It was one of a row of houses that looked very much alike, which, itself, was one of four sides of a square. In the centre of the square was a park-like space, a garden, really. In this garden were several tennis courts, with plenty of space, also, for nurses and children. There are many such squares in London, and they help to make the British capital a delightful place in which to live.

As he went in, Harry saw a lot of the younger men who lived in the square playing tennis. It was still broad daylight, although, at home, dusk would have fallen. But this was England at the end of July and the beginning of August, and the light of day would hold until ten o'clock or thereabout. That was one of the things that had helped to reconcile Harry to living in England. He loved the long evenings and the chance they gave to get plenty of sport and exercise after school hours.

The school that he and Dick attended was not far away; they went to it each day. A great many of the boys boarded at the school, but there were plenty who, like Dick and Harry, did not. But school was over now, for the time. The summer holidays had just begun.

At the table there was much talk of the war that was in the air. But Mr. Fleming did not even yet believe that war was sure.

"They'll patch it up," he said, confidently. "They can't be so mad as to set the whole world ablaze over a little scrap like the trouble between Austria and Servia."

"Would it affect your business, dear?" asked Mrs. Fleming. "If there really should be war, I mean ?"

"I don't think so," said he. "I might have to make a flying trip home, but I'd be back. Come on - time for us to go. What are you going to do, boy? Going over to Grenfel's, aren't you ?"

"Yes, father," said Harry.

"All right. Get home early. Good-night!"

A good many of the boys were already there when Dick and Harry reached Grenfel's house. The troop - the Forty-second, of London - was a comparatively small one, having only three patrols. But nearly all of them were present, and the scout-master took them out into his garden.

"I'm going to change the order a bit," he said, gravely. "I want to do some talking, and then I expect to answer questions. Boys, Germany has declared war on Russia. There are reports already of fighting on the border between France and Germany. And there seems to be an idea that the Germans are certain to strike at France through Belgium. I may not be here very long - I may have to turn over the troop to another scoutmaster. So I want to have a long talk to-night." There was a dismayed chorus.

"What? You going away, sir? Why?"

But Harry did not join. He saw the quiet blaze in John

George Durston

Grenfel's eyes, and he thought he knew.

"I've volunteered for foreign service already," Grenfel explained. "I saw a little fighting in the Boer war, you know. And I may be useful. So I thought I'd get my application in directly. If I go, I'll probably go quietly and quickly. And there may be no other chance for me to say good-bye."

'Then you think England will be drawn in, sir?" asked Leslie Franklin, leader of the patrol to which Dick and Harry belonged, the Royal Blues.

"I'm afraid so," said Grenfels grimly. "There's just a chance still, but that's all - the ghost of a chance, you might call it. I think it might be as well if I explained a little of what's back of all this trouble. Want to listen? If you do, I'll try. And if I'm not making myself clear, ask all the questions you like."

There was a chorus of assent. Grenfel sat in the middle, the scouts ranged about him in a circle. "In the first place," he began, "this Servian business is only an excuse. I'm not defending the Servians - I'm taking no sides between Servia and Austria. Here in England we don't care about that, because we know that if that hadn't started the war, something else would have been found.

"England wants peace. And it seems that, every so often, she has to fight for it. It was so when the Duke of Marlborough won his battles at Blenheim and Ramillies and Malplaquet. Then France was the strongest nation in Europe. And she tried to crush the others and dominate everything. If she had, she would have been strong enough, after her victories, to fight us over here - to invade England. So we went into that war, more than two hundred years ago, not because we hated France, but to make a real peace possible. And it lasted a long time.

"Then, after the French revolution, there was Napoleon. Again France, under him, was the strongest nation in Europe. He conquered Germany, and Austria, Italy and Spain, the

Netherlands. And he tried to conquer England, so that France could rule the world. But Nelson beat his fleet at Trafalgar -"

"Hurrah!" interrupted Dick, carried away. "Three cheers for Nelson!"

Grenfel smiled as the cheers were given.

"Even after Trafalgar," he went on, "Napoleon hoped to conquer England. He had massed a great army near Boulogne, ready to send it across the channel. And so we took the side of the weaker nations again. All Europe, led by England, rose against Napoleon. And you know what happened. He was beaten finally at Waterloo. And so there was peace again in Europe for a long time, with no one nation strong enough to dictate to all the others." But then Germany began to rise. She beat Austria, and that made her the strongest German country. Then she beat France, in 1870, and that gave her her start toward being the strongest nation on the continent.

"And then, I believe - and so do most Englislmen - she began to be jealous of England. She wanted our colonies. She began, finally, to build a great navy. For years we have had to spend great sums of money to keep our fleet stronger than hers. And she made an alliance with Austria and Italy. Because of that France and Russia made an alliance, too, and we had to be friendly with them. And now it looks to me as if Germany thought she saw a chance to beat France and Russia. Perhaps she thinks that we won't fight, on account of the trouble in Ireland. And what we English fear is that, if she wins, she will take Belgium and Holland. Then she would be so close to our coasts that we would never be safe. We would have to be prepared always for invasion. So, you see, it seems to me that we are facing the same sort of danger we have faced before. Only this time it is Germany, instead of France, that we shall have to fight - if we do fight."

"If the Germans go through Belgium, will that mean that we shall fight?" asked Leslie Franklin.

"Almost certainly, yes," said Grenfel. "And it is through Belgium that Germany has her best chance to strike at France. So you see how serious things are. I don't want to go into all the history that is back of all this. I just want you to understand what England's interest is. If we make war, it will be a war of self-defence. Suppose you owned a house. And suppose the house next door caught fire. You would try to put out that fire, wouldn't you, to save your own house from being burned up? Well, that's England's position. If the Germans held Belgium or Holland - and they would hold both, if they beat France and Russia - England would then be in just as much danger as your house would be. So if we fight, it will be to put out the German fire in the house next door.

"Now I want you to understand one thing. I'm talking as an Englishman. A German would tell you all this in a very different way. I don't like the people who are always slandering their enemies. Germany has her reasons for acting as she does. I think her reasons are wrong. But the Germans believe that they are right. We can respect even people who are wrong if they themselves believe that they are right. There may be two sides to this quarrel. And Germans, even if they are to be our enemies, may be just as patriotic, just as devoted to their country, as we are. Never forget that, no matter what may happen."

He stopped then, waiting for questions. None came.

"Then you understand pretty well?" he asked. There was a murmur of assent from the whole circle.

"All right, then," he said. "Now there's work for Scouts to do. Be prepared! That's our motto, isn't it? Suppose there's war. Franklin, what's your idea of what the Boy Scouts would be able to do?"

"I suppose those who are old enough could volunteer, sir," said Franklin, doubtfully. "I can't think of anything else -"

"Time enough for that later," said Grenfel, with a short laugh. "England may have to call boys to the colors before she's done, if she once starts to fight. But long before that time comes, there will be a great work for the organization we all love and honor. Work that won't be showy, work that will be very hard. Boys, everyone in England, man and woman and child will have work to do! And we, who are organized, and whose motto Be Prepared, ought to be able to show what stuff there is in us.

"Think of all the places that must be guarded. The waterworks, the gas tanks, the railroads that lead to the seaports and that will be used by the troops."

A startled burst of exclamations answered him. "Why, there won't be any fighting in England, sir, will there?" asked Dick Mercer, in surprise.

"We all hope not," said Grenfel. "But that's not what I mean. It doesn't take an army to destroy a railroad. One man with a bomb and a time fuse attached to it can blow up a culvert and block a whole line so that precious hours might be lost in getting troops aboard a transport. One man could blow up a waterworks or a gas tank or cut an important telegraph or telephone wire!"

"You mean that there will be Germans here trying to hurt England any way they can, don't you sir? asked Harry Fleming.

"I mean exactly that," said Grenfel. "We don't know this - we can't be sure of it. But we've got good reason to believe that there are a great many Germans here, seemingly peaceable enough, who are regularly in the pay of the German government as spies. We don't know the German plans. But there is no reason, so far as we know, why their great Zeppelin airships shouldn't come sailing over England, to drop bombs down where they can do the most harm. There is nothing except our own vigilance to keep these spies, even if they have to work alone, from doing untold damage!"

'We could be useful as sentries, then?" said Leslie Franklin. He drew a deep breath. "I never thought of things like that, sir! I'm just beginning to see how useful we really might be. We could do a lot of things instead of soldiers, couldn't we? So that they would be free to go and fight?"

"Yes," answered the scoutmaster. "And I can tell you now that the National Scout Council has always planned to 'Be Prepared!' It decided, a long time ago, what should be done in case of war. A great many troops will be offered to the War Department to do odd jobs. They will carry messages and dispatches. They will act as clerks, so far as they can. They will patrol the railways and other places that ought to be under guard, where soldiers can be spared if we take their places. So far as such things can be planned, they have been planned.

"But most of the ways in which we can be useful haven't showed themselves, at all yet. They will develop, if war comes. We shall have to be alert and watchful, and do whatever there is to be done..."

"Who will be scoutmaster, sir. if you go to the war?" asked Harry.

"I'm not quite sure," said Grenfel. "We haven't decided yet. But it will be someone you can trust - be sure of that. And I think I needn't say that if you scouts have any real regard for me you will show it best by serving as loyally and as faithfully under him as you have under me. I shall be with you in spirit, no matter where I am. Now it's, getting late. I think we'd better break up for tonight. We will make a special order, too, for the present. Every scout in the troop will report at scout headquarters until further notice, every day, at nine o'clock in the morning.

"I think we'll have to make up our minds not to play many games for the time that is coming. There is real work ahead of us if war comes - work just as real and just as hard, in its way, as if we were all going to fight for England. Everyone cannot fight, but the ones who stay at home and do the work that comes to their hands will serve England just as loyally as if they were on the firing line. Now up, all of you! Three cheers for King George!"

They were given with a will - and Harry Fleming joined in as heartily as any of them. He was as much of an American as he had ever been, but something in him responded with a strange thrill to England's need, as Grenfel had expressed it. After all, England had been and was the mother country. England and America had fought, in their time, and America had won, but now, for a hundred years, there had been peace between them. And he and these English boys were of the same blood and the same language, binding them very closely together. "Blood is thicker than water, after all!" he thought.

Then every scout there shook hands with John Grenfel. He smiled as he greeted them.

"I hope this will pass over," he said, "and that we'll do together during this vacation all the things we've planned to do. But if we can't, and if I'm called away, good-bye! Do your duty as scouts, and I'll know it somehow! And, in case I don't see you again, good-bye!"

"You're going to stand with us, then, Fleming?" he said, as Harry came up to shake hands. "Good boy! We're of one blood, we English and you Americans. We've had our quarrels, but relatives always do quarrel. And you'll not be asked, as a scout here, to do anything an American shouldn't do."

Then it was over. They were out in the street. In the distance newsboys were yelling their extra still. Many people were out, something unusual in that quiet neighborhood. And suddenly one of the scouts lifted his voice, and in a moment they were all singing:

Rule, rule, Britannia!
Britannia rules the waves!

Britons never, never, never shall be slaves!

Scores of voices swelled the chorus, joining the fresh young voices of the scouts. And then someone started that swinging march song that had leaped into popularity at the time of the Boer War, Soldiers of the Queen. The words were trifling, but there was a fine swing to the music, and it was not the words that counted - it was the spirit of those who sang.

As he marched along with the others Harry noticed one thing. In a few hours the whole appearance of the streets had changed. From every house, in the still night air, drooped a Union Jack. The flag was everywhere; some houses had flung out half a dozen to the wind.

Harry was seeing a sight, that once seen, can never be forgotten. He was seeing a nation aroused, preparing to fight. If war came to England it would be no war decreed by a few men. It would be a war proclaimed by the people themselves, demanded by them. The nation was stirring; it was casting off the proverbial lethargy and indifference of the English. Even here, in this usually quiet suburb of London, the home of business and professional men who were comfortably well off, the stirring of the spirit of England was evident. And suddenly the song of the scouts and those who had joined them was drowned out by a new noise, sinister, threatening. It was the angry note that is raised by a mob.

Leslie Franklin took command at once. "Here, we must see what's wrong!" he cried. "Scouts, attention! Fall in! Double quick - follow me!"

He ran in the direction of the sound, and they followed. Five minutes brought them to the scene of the disturbance. They reached a street of cheaper houses and small shops. About one of these a crowd was surging, made up largely of young men of the lower class, for in West Kensington, as in all parts of London, the homes of the rich and of the poor rub one another's elbows in easy familiarity. The crowd seemed to be trying to break in the door of this shop. Already all the glass of the show windows had been broken, and from within there came guttural cries of alarm and anger.

"It's Dutchy's place!" cried Dick Mercer. "He's a German, and they're trying to smash his place up!"

"Halt!" cried Franklin. He gathered the scouts about him. "This won't do," he said, angry spots of color showing on his cheek bones. "No one's gone for the police - or, if they have, this crowd of muckers will smash everything up and maybe hurt the old Dutchman before the Bobbies get here. Form together now - and when I give the word, go through! Once we get between them and the shop, we can stop them. Maybe they won't know who we are at first, and our uniforms may stop them."

"Now!" he said, a moment later. And, with a shout, the scouts charged through the little mob in a body.

They had no trouble in getting through. A few determined people, knowing just what they mean to do, can always overcome a greater number of disorganized ones. That is why disciplined troops can conquer five times their number of rioters or savages. And so in a moment they reached the shop.

"Let us in! We're here to protect you!" cried Franklin to old Schmidt, who was cowering within, with his wife. Then he turned to the rioters, who, getting over their first surprise, were threatening again.

"For shame!" he cried. "Do you think you're doing anything for England? War's not declared yet - and, if it was, you might better be looking for German soldiers to shoot at than trying to hurt an old man who never did anyone any harm!"

There was a threatening noise from the crowd, but Franklin was undismayed.

"You'll have to get through us to reach them !" he cried. "We -"

But he was interrupted. A whistle sounded. The next moment the police were there.

CHAPTER III

PICKED FOR SERVICE

The coming of the police cleared the little crowd of would-be rioters away in no time. There were only three or four of the Bobbies, but they were plenty. A smiling sergeant came up to Franklin.

"More of your Boy Scout work, sir?" he said, pleasantly. "I heard you standing them off! That was very well done. If we can depend on you to help us all over London, we'll have an easier job than we looked for."

"We saw a whole lot of those fellows piling up against the shop here," said Franklin. "So of course we pitched in. We couldn't let anything like that happen."

"There'll be a lot of it at first, I'm afraid, sir," said the sergeant. "Still, it won't last. If all we hear is true, they'll be taking a lot of those young fellows away and giving them some real fighting to do to keep them quiet."

"Well, we'll help whenever we can, sergeant," said Franklin. "If the inspector thinks it would be a good thing to have the shops that are kept by Germans watched, I'm quite sure it can be arranged. If there's war I suppose a lot of you policemen will go?"

"We'll supply our share, sir," said the sergeant. "I'm expecting

George Durston

orders any minute - I'm a reservist myself. Coldstream Guards, sir."

"Congratulations!" said Franklin. He spoke a little wistfully. "I wonder if they'll let me go? I think I'm old enough! Well, can we help any more here tonight?"

"No, thank you, sir. You've done very well as it is. Pity all the lads don't belong to the Boy Scouts. We'd have less trouble, I'll warrant. I'll just leave a man here to watch the place. But they won't be back. They don't mean any real harm, as it is. It's just their spirits - and their being a bit thoughtless, you know."

"All right," said Franklin. "Glad we came along. Good-night, sergeant. Fall in! March!"

There was a cheer from the crowd that had gathered to watch the disturbance as the scouts move away. A hundred yards from the scene of what might have been a tragedy, except for their prompt action, the scouts dispersed. Dick, Mercer and Harry Fleming naturally enough, since they lived so close to one another, went home together.

"That was quick work," said Harry.

"Yes. I'm glad we got there," said Dick. "Old Dutchy's all right - he doesn't seem like a German. But I think it would be a good thing if they did catch a few of the others and scrag them!"

"No, it wouldn't," said Harry soberly. "Don't get to feeling that way, Dick. Suppose you were living in Berlin. You wouldn't want a lot of German roughs to come and destroy your house or your shop and handle you that way, would you?"

"It's not the same thing," said Dick, stubbornly. "They're foreigners."

"But you'd be a foreigner if you were over there!" said Harry, with a laugh.

"I suppose I would," said Dick. "I never thought of that! Just the same, I bet Mr. Grenfel was right. London's full of spies. Isn't that an awful idea, Harry? You can't tell who's a spy and who isn't!"

"No, but you can be pretty sure that the man you suspect isn't," suggested Harry, sagely. "A real spy wouldn't let you find it out very easily. I can see one thing and that is a whole lot of perfectly harmless people are going to be arrested as spies before this war is very old, if it does come! We don't want to be mixed up in that, Dick - we scouts. If we think a man's doing anything suspicious, we'll have to be very sure before we denounce him, or else we won't be any use."

"It's better for a few people to be arrested by mistake than to let a spy keep on spying, isn't it?"

"I suppose so, but we don't want to be like the shepherd's boy who used to try to frighten people by calling 'Wolf! Wolf!' when there wasn't any wolf. You know what happened to him. When a wolf really did come no one believed him. Wo want to look before we leap."

"I suppose you're right, Harry. Oh, I do hope we can really be of some use! If I can't go to the war, I'd like to think I'd had something to do - that I'd helped when my country needed me!"

"If you feel like that you'll be able to help, all right," said Harry. "I feel that way, too not that I want to fight. I wouldn't want to do that for any country but my own. But I would like to be able to know that I'd had something to do with all that's going to be done."

"I think it's fine for you to be like that," said Dick. "I think there isn't so much difference between us, after all, even if you are American and I'm English. Well, here we are again. I'll see you in the morning, I suppose?"

"Right oh! I'll come around for you early. Goodnight!"

"Goodnight!"

Neither of them really doubted for a moment that war was coming. It was in the air. The attack on the little shop that they had helped to avert was only one of many, although there was no real rioting in London. Such scenes were simply the result of excitement, and no great harm was done anywhere. But the tension of which such attacks were the result was everywhere. For the next three days there was very little for anyone to do.

Everyone was waiting. France and Germany were at war; the news came that the Germans had invaded Luxembourg, and were crossing the Belgian border.

And then, on Tuesday night, came the final news. England had declared war. For the moment the news seemed to stun everyone. It had been expected, and still it came as a surprise. But then London rose to the occasion. There was no hysterical cheering and shouting; everything was quiet. Harry Fleming saw a wonderful sight a whole people aroused and determined. There was no foolish boasting; no one talked of a British general eating his Christmas dinner in Berlin. But even Dick Mercer, excitable and erratic as he had always been, seemed to have undergone a great change.

"My father's going to the war," he told Harry on Wednesday morning. He spoke very seriously. "He was a captain in the Boer War, you know, so he knows something about soldiering. He thinks he'll be taken, though he's a little older than most of the men who'll go. He'll be an officer, of course. And he says I've got to look after the mater when he's gone."

"You can do it, too," said Harry, surprised, despite himself, by the change in his chum's manner. "You seem older than I now, Dick, and I've always thought you were a kid!"

"The pater says we've all got to be men, now," said Dick, steadily. "The mater cried a bit when he said he was going - but I think she must have known all the time he was going. Because when he told us - we were at the breakfast table - she sort of cried a little, and then she stopped.

"I've got everything ready for you,' she said.

"And he looked at her, and smiled. 'So you knew I was going?' he asked her. And she nodded her head, and he got up and kissed her. I never saw him do that before he never did that before, when I was looking on," Dick concluded seriously. "I hope he'll come back all right, Dick," said Harry. "It's hard, old chap!"

"I wouldn't have him stay home for anything!" said Dick, fiercely. "And I will do my share! You see if I don't! I don't care what they want me to do! I'll run errands - I'll sweep out the floors in the War Office, so that some man can go to war! I'll do anything!"

Somehow Harry realized in that moment how hard it was going to be to beat a country where even the boys felt like that! The change in the usually thoughtless, light-hearted Dick impressed him more than anything else had been able to do with the real meaning of what had come about so suddenly. And he was thankful, too, all at once, that in America the fear and peril of War were so remote. It was glorious, it was thrilling, but it was terrible, too. He wondered how many of the scouts he knew, and how many of those in school would lose their fathers or their brothers in this war that was beginning. Truly, there is no argument for peace that can compare with war itself! Yet how slowly we learn!

Grenfel had gone, and the troop was now in charge of a new scoutmaster, Francis Wharton. Mr. Wharton was a somewhat older man. At first sight he didn't look at all like the man to lead a group of scouts, but that, as it turned out, was due to physical infirmities. One foot had been amputated at the time of the Boer War, in which he had served with Grenfel. As a result he was incapacitated from active service, although, as the scouts soon learned, he had begged to be allowed to go in spite of it. He appeared at the scout headquarters, the pavilion of a small local cricket club, on Wednesday morning.

"I don't know much about this - more shame to me," he said, cheerfully, standing up to address the boys. "But I think we can make a go of it - think we'll be able to do something for the Empire, boys. My old friend John Grenfel told me a little; he said you'd pull me through. These are war times and you'll have to do for me what many a company in the army does for a young officer."

They gave him a hearty cheer that was a promise in itself.

"I can tell you I felt pretty bad when I found they wouldn't let me go to the front," he went on. "It seemed hard to have to sit back and read the newspapers when I knew I ought to be doing some of the work. But then Grenfel told me about you boys, and what you meant to do, and I felt better. I saw that there was a chance for me to help, after all. So here I am. These are times when ordinary routine doesn't matter so much you can understand that. Grenfel put the troop at the disposal of the commander at Ealing. And his first request was that I should send two scouts to him at once. Franklin, I believe you are the senior patrol leader? Yes? Then I shall appoint you assistant scoutmaster, as Mr. Greene has not returned from his holiday in France. Will you suggest the names of two scouts for this service?"

Franklin immediately went up to the new scoutmaster, and they spoke together quietly, while a buzz of excited talk rose among the scouts. Who would be honored by the first chance? Every scout there wanted to hear his name called.

"I think they'll take me, for one," said Ernest Graves. He was one of the patrol to which both Harry Fleming and Dick Mercer belonged, and the biggest and oldest scout of the troop, except for Leslie Franklin. He had felt for some time that he should be a patrol leader. Although he excelled in games, and was unquestionably a splendid scout, Graves was not popular, for some reason, among his fellows. He was not exactly unpopular, either; but there was a little resentment at his habit of pushing himself forward.

"I don't see why you should go more than anyone else, Graves," said young Mercer. "I think they'd take the ones who are quickest. We're probably wanted for messenger work."

"Well, I'm the oldest. I ought to have first chance," said Graves.

But the discussion was ended abruptly.

"Fleming! Mercer!" called Mr. Wharton.

They stepped forward, their hands raised in the scout salute, awaiting the scoutmaster's orders. "You will proceed at once, by rail, to Ealing," he said. "There you will report at the barracks, handing this note to the officer of the guard. He will then conduct you to the adjutant or the officer in command, from whom you will take your orders."

"Yes, sir," said both scouts. Their eyes were afire with enthusiasm. But as they passed toward the door, Dick Mercer's quick ears caught a sullen murmur from Graves.

"He's making a fine start," he heard him say to Fatty Wells, who was a great admirer of his. "Picking out an AMERICAN! Why, we're not even sure that he'll be loyal! Did you ever hear of such a thing?"

"You shut up!" cried Dick, fiercely, turning on Graves. "He's as loyal as anyone else! We know as much about him as we do about you, anyhow - or more! You may be big, but when we get back I'll make you take that back or fight -"

"Come on," said Harry, pulling Dick along with him. "You mustn't start quarreling now - it's time for all of us to stand together, Dick. I don't care what he says, anyhow."

He managed to get his fiery chum outside, and they hurried along, at the scout pace, running and walking alternately, toward the West Kensington station of the Underground Railway. They were in their khaki scout uniforms, and several people turned to smile admiringly at them. The newspapers had already announced that the Boy Scouts had turned out unanimously to do whatever service they could, and it was a time when women - and it was mostly women who were in the streets - were disposed to display their admiration of those who were working for the country very freely.

They had little to say to one another as they hurried along; their pace was such as to make it wise for them to save their breath. But when they reached the station they found they had some minutes to wait for a train, and they sat down on the platform to get their breath. They had already had one proof of the difference made by a state of war.

Harry stopped at the ticket window.

"Two-third class - for Ealing," he said, putting down the money. But the agent only smiled, having seen their uniforms.

"On the public service ?" he questioned.

"Yes," said Harry, rather proudly.

"Then you don't need tickets," said the agent. "Got my orders this morning. No one in uniform has to pay. Go right through, and ride first-class, if you like. You'll find plenty of officers riding that way."

"That's fine!" said Dick. "It makes it seem as if we were really of some use, doesn't it, Harry?"

"Yes," answered Harry. "But, Dick, I've been thinking of what you said to Graves. What did you mean when you told him you knew more about me than you did about him? Hasn't he lived here a long time?"

"No, and there's a little mystery about him. Don't you know it?"

"Never heard of such a thing, Dick. You see, I haven't been here so very long and he was in the patrol when I joined.",

"Oh, yes, so he was! Well, I'll tell you, then. You know he's studying to be an engineer, at the Polytechnic. And he lives at a boarding house, all by himself. Not a regular boarding house, exactly. He boards with Mrs. Johnson, you know. Her husband died a year or two ago, and didn't leave her very much money. He hasn't any father or mother, but he always seems to have plenty of money. And he can play all sorts of games, but he won't do them up right. He says he doesn't care anything about cricket!"

"How old is he?"

"Sixteen, but he's awfully big and strong."

"He certainly is. He looks older than that, to me. Have you ever noticed anything funny about the way he talks?"

"No. Why? Have you?"

"I'm not sure. But sometimes it seems to me he talks more like the people do in a book than you and I do. I wonder why he doesn't like me?" pondered Harry.

"Oh, he likes you as well as he does anyone, Harry. He didn't mean anything, I fancy, when he said that about your being chosen just now. He was squiffed because Mr. Wharton didn't take him, that's all. He thinks he ought to be ahead of everyone."

"Well, I didn't ask to be chosen. I'm glad I was, of course, but I didn't expect to be. I think perhaps Leslie Franklin asked Mr. Wharton to take me."

"Of course he did! Why shouldn't he?"

Just then the coming of the train cut them short. From almost every window men in uniform looked out. A few of the soldiers laughed at their scout garb, but most of them only smiled gravely, and as if they were well pleased. The two scouts made for the nearest compartment, and found, when they were in it, that it was a first-class carriage, already containing two young officers who were smoking and chatting together.

"Hullo, young 'uns!" said one of the officers. "Off to the war?"

They both laughed, which Harry rather resented. "We're under orders, sir," he said, politely. "But, of course, they won't let us Scouts go to the war."

"Don't rag them, Cecil," said the other officer. "They're just the sort we need. Going to Ealing, boys?"

Harry checked Dick's impulsive answer with a quick snatch at his elbow. He looked his questioner straight in the eye.

"We weren't told to answer any questions, sir," he said.

Both the officers roared with laughter, but they sobered quickly, and the one who had asked the question flushed a little.

"I beg your pardon, my boy," he said. "The question is withdrawn. You're perfectly right - and you're setting us an example by taking things seriously. This war isn't going to be a lark. But you can tell me a few things. You're scouts, I see. I was myself, once - before I went to Sandhurst. What troop and patrol?"

Dick told him, and the officer nodded.

"Good work!" he said. "The scouts are going to turn out and help, he? That's splendid! There'll be work enough to go all around, never you fear."

"If, by any chance, you should be going to Ealing Barracks," said the first officer, rather shyly, "and we should get off the train when you do, there's no reason why you shouldn't let us drive you out, is there? We're going there, and I don't mind telling you that we've just finished a two hour leave to go and say good-bye to - to -"

His voice broke a little at that. In spite of his light-hearted manner and his rather chaffing tone, he couldn't help remembering that good-bye. He was going to face whatever fate might come, but thoughts of those he might not see again could not be prevented from obtruding themselves.

"Shut up, Cecil," said the other. "We've said good-bye - that's the end of it! We've got other things to think of now. Here we are!"

The train pulled into Ealing station. Here the evidences of war and the warlike preparations were everywhere. The platforms were full of soldiers, laughing, jostling one another, saluting the officers who passed among them. And Harry, as he and Dick followed the officers toward the gate, saw one curious thing. A sentry stood by the railway official who was taking up tickets, and two or three times he stopped and questioned civilian passengers. Two of these, moreover, he ordered into the ticket office, where, as he went by, Harry saw an officer, seated at a desk, examining civilians.

Ealing, as a place where many troops were quartered, was

plainly very much under martial law. And outside the station it was even more military. Soldiers were all about and automobiles were racing around, too. And there were many women and children here, to bid farewell to the soldiers who were going - where? No one knew. That was the mystery of the morning. Everyone understood that the troops were off; that they had their orders. But not even the officers themselves knew where, it seemed.

"Here we are - here's a car!" said the officer called Cecil. "Jump aboard, young 'uns! We know where you're going, right enough. Might as well save some time."

And so in a few minutes they reached the great barracks. Here the bustle that had been so marked about the station was absent. All was quiet. They were challenged by a sentry and Harry asked for the officer of the guard. When he came he handed him Wharton's letter. They were told to wait - outside. And then, in a few minutes, the officer returned, passed them through, and turned them over to an orderly, who took them to the room where Colonel Throckmorton, who was seemingly in charge of important affairs, received them. He returned their salute, then bent a rather stern gaze upon them before he spoke.

CHAPTER IV

THE HOUSE OF THE HELIOGRAPH

"You know your way about London?" he asked.

"Yes, sir," said Harry.

"I shall have messages for you to carry," said the colonel, then. "Now I want to explain, so that you will understand the importance of this, why you are going to be allowed to do this work. This war has come suddenly - but we are sure that the enemy has expected it for a long time, and has made plans accordingly.

"There are certain matters so important, so secret, that we are afraid to trust them to the telephone, the telegraph - even the post, if that were quick enough! In a short time we shall have weeded out all the spies. Until then we have to exercise the greatest care. And it has been decided to accept the offer of Boy Scouts because the spies we feel we must guard against are less likely to suspect boys than men. I am going to give you some dispatches now - what they are is a secret. You take them to Major French, at Waterloo station."

He stopped, apparently expecting them to speak. But neither said anything.

"No questions?" he asked, sternly.

George Durston

"No - no, sir," said Dick. "We're to take the dispatches to Major French, at Waterloo? That all, is it, sir? And then to come back here?"

The colonel nodded approvingly.

"Yes, that's all," he said. "Except for this. Waterloo station is closed to all civilians. You will require a word to pass the sentries. No matter what you see, once you are inside, you are not to describe it. You are to tell no one, not even your parent - what you do or what you see. That is all," and he nodded in dismissal.

They made their way out and back to the railway station. And Dick seemed a little disappointed.

"I don't think this is much to be doing!" he grumbled.

But Harry's eyes were glistening.

"Don't you see ?" he said, lowering his voice so they could not be overheard. "We know something now that probably even a lot of the soldiers don't know! They're mobilizing. If they are going to be sent from Waterloo it must mean that they're going to Southampton - and that means that they will reach France. That's what we'll see at Waterloo station - troops entraining to start the trip to France. They're going to fight over there. Everyone is guessing at that - a lot of people thought most of the army would be sent to the East Coast. But that can't be so, you see. If it was, they would be starting from King's Cross and Liverpool street stations, not from Waterloo."

"Oh, I never thought of that!" said Dick, brightening.

When they got on the train at Ealing they were lucky enough to get a compartment to themselves, since at that time more people were coming to Ealing than were leaving it. Dick began at once to give vent to his wonder.

"How many of them do you suppose are going?" he cried. "Who will be in command? Sir John Frencli, I think. Lord Kitchener is to be War Minister, they say, and stay in London. I bet they whip those bally Germans until they don't know where they are -"

"Steady on!" said Harry, smiling, but a little concerned, none the less. "Dick, don't talk that! You don't know who may be listening!"

"Why, Harry! No one can hear us - we're alone in the carriage!"

"I know, but we don't know who's in the next one or whether they ean hear through or not. The wall isn't very thick, you know. We can't be too careful. I don't think anyone knows what we're doing but there isn't any reason why we should take any risk at all."

"No, of course not. You're right, Harry," said Dick, a good deal abashed. "I'll try to keep quiet after this."

"I wonder why there are two of us," said Dick presently, in a whisper. "I should think one would be enough."

"I think we've both got just the same papers to carry," said Harry, also in a whisper. "You see, if one of us gets lost, or anything happens to his papers, the other will probably get through all right. At least it looks that way to me."

"Harry," said Dick, after a pause, "I've got an idea. Suppuse we separate and take different ways to get to Waterloo? Wouldn't that make it safer? We could meet there and go back to Ealing together."

"That's a good idea, Dick," said Harry. He didn't think that their present errand was one of great importance, in spite of what Colonel Throckmorton had said. He thought it more likely that they were being tried out and tested, so that the colonel might draw his own conclusions as to how far he might safely trust them in the future. But he repressed his inclination to smile at this sudden excess of caution on Dick's part. It was a move in the right direction, certainly.

"Yes, we'll do that," he said. "I'll walk across the bridge, and you can take the tube under the river from the Monument."

They followed that plan, and met without incident at the station. Here more than ever the fact of war was in evidence. A considerable space in and near the station had been roped off and sentries refused to allow any to pass who could not prove that they had a right to do so. The ordinary peaceful vocation of the great terminal was entirely suspended.

"Anything happen to you ?" asked Harry with a smile. "I nearly got run over - but that was my own fault."

"No, nothing. I saw Graves. And he wanted to know what I was doing."

"What did you tell him?"

"Nothing. I said, 'Don't you wish you knew?' And he got angry, and said he didn't care."

"It wasn't any of his business. You did right," said Harry.

They had to wait a few moments to see Major French, who was exceedingly busy. They need no one to tell them what was going on. At the platform trains were waiting, and, even while they looked on, one after another drew out, loaded with soldiers. The windows were whitewashed, so that, once the doors of the compartments were closed, none could see who was inside. There was no cheering, which seemed strange at first, but it was so plain that this was a precautionary measure that the boys understood it easily enough. Finally Major French, an energetic, sunburned man, who looked as if he hadn't slept for days, came to them. They handed him the papers they carried. He glanced at them, signed receipts which he handed to them, and then frowned for a moment.

"I think I'll let you take a message to Colonel Throckmorton for me," he said, then, giving them a kindly smile. "It will be a verbal message. You are to repeat what I tell you to him without a change. And I suppose I needn't tell you that you must give it to no one else?"

"No, sir." they chorused.

"Very well, then. You will tell him that trains will be waiting below Surbiton, at precisely ten o'clock tonight. Runways will be built to let the men climb the embankment, and they can entrain there. You will remember that ?"

"Yes, sir."

"You might as well understand what it's all about," said the major. "You see, we're moving a lot of troops. And it is of the utmost importance for the enemy to know all about the movement and, of course, just as important for us to keep them from learning what they want to know. So we are covering the movement as well as we can. Even if they learn some of the troops that are going, we want to keep them from finding out everything. Their spy system is wonderfully complete and we have to take every precaution that is possible. It is most important that you deliver this message to Colonel Throckmorton. Repeat it to me exactly," he commanded.

They did so, and, seemingly satisfied, he let them go. But just as they were leaving, he called them back.

"You'd go back by the underground, I suppose," he said. "I'm not sure that you can get through for the line is likely to be taken over, temporarily, at any moment. Take a taxicab - I'll send an orderly with you to put you aboard. Don't pay the man anything; we are keeping a lot of them outside on government service, and they get their pay from the authorities."

The orderly led them to the stand, some distance from the station, where the cabs stood in a long row, and spoke to the driver of the one at the head of the rank. In a moment the motor was started, and they were off.

The cab had a good engine, and it made good time. But after a little while Harry noticed with some curiosity that the route they were taking was not the most direct one. He rapped on the window glass and spoke to the driver about it.

"Got to go round, sir," the man explained. "Roads are all torn up the straight way, sir. Won't take much longer, sir."

Harry accepted the explanation. Indeed, it seemed reasonable enough. But some sixth sense warned him to keep his eyes open. And at last he decided that there could be no excuse for the way the cab was proceeding. It seemed to him that they were going miles out of the way, and decidedly in the wrong direction. He did not know London as well as a boy who had lived there all his life would have done. But his scout training had given him a remarkable ability to keep his bearings. And it needed no special knowledge to realize that the sun was on the wrong side of the cab for a course that was even moderately straight for Ealing.

They had swung well around, as a matter of fact, into a northwestern suburban section, and once he had seen a maze of railway tracks that meant, he was almost sure that they were passing near Willisden Junction. Only a few houses appeared in the section through which the cab was now racing and pavements were not frequent. He spoke to Dick: in a whisper.

"There's something funny here," he said. "But, no matter what happens pretend you think it's all right. Let anyone who speaks to us think we're foolish. It will be easier for us to get away then. And keep your eyes wide open, if we stop anywhere, so that you will be sure to know the place again!"

"Right!" said Dick.

Just then the cab, caught in a rutty road where the going was very heavy, and there was a slight upgrade in addition, to make it worse, slowed up considerably. And Dick, looking out the window on his side, gave a stifled exclamation.

"Look there, Harry!" he said. "Do you see the sun flashing on something on the roof of that house over there? What do you suppose that is?"

"Whew!" Harry whistled, "You ought to know that, Dick! A heliograph - field telegraph. Morse code - or some code - made by flashes. The sun catches a mirror or some sort of reflector, and it's just like a telegraph instrument, with dots and dashes, except that you work by sight instead of by sound. That is queer. Try to mark just where the house is, and so will I."

The cab turned, while they were still looking, and removed the house where the signalling was being done from their line of vision. But in a few moments there was a loud report that startled the scouts until they realized that a front tire had blown out. The driver stopped at once, and descended, seemingly much perturbed. And Harry and Dick, piling out to inspect the damage, started when they saw that they had stopped just outside the mysterious house.

"I'll fix that in a jiffy," said the driver, and began jacking up the wheel. But, quickly as he stripped off the deflated tire, he was not so quick that Harry failed to see that the blow-out had been caused by a straight cut - not at all the sort of tear produced by a jagged stone or a piece of broken glass. He said nothing of his discovery, however, and a moment later he looked up to face a young man in the uniform of an officer of the British territorial army. This young man had keen, searching blue eyes, and very blond hair. His upper lip was closely shaven, but it bore plain evidence that within a few days it had sported a moustache.

"Well," said the officer, "what are you doing here?"

The driver straightened up as if in surprise. "Blow-out, sir," he said, touching his cap. "I'm carrying these young gentlemen from Waterloo to Ealing, sir. Had to come around on account of the roads."

"You've have your way lost, my man. Why not admit it?" said the officer, showing his white teeth in a smile. He turned to Harry an Dick. "Boy Scouts, I see," he commented. "You carry orders concerning the movement of troops from Ealing? They are to entrain - where?"

"Near Croydon, sir, on the Brighton and South Coast Line," said Harry, lifting his innocent eyes to his questioner.

"So! They go to Dover, then, I suppose - no, perhaps to Folkestone - - oh, what matter? Hurry up with your tire, my man!"

He watched them still as the car started. Then he went back to the house.

"Whatever did you tell him that whopper about Croydon for?" whispered Dick. "I wasn't going to tell him anything -"

"Then he might have tried to make us," answered Harry, also in a whisper. "Did you notice anything queer about him ?"

"Why, no -"

"You have your way lost!' Would any Englishman say that, Dick? And wouldn't a German? You've studied German. Translate 'You've lost your way' into German. 'Du hast dein weg - ' See? He was a German spy!"

"Oh, Harry! I believe you're right! But why didn't we -"

"Try to arrest him? There may have been a dozen others there, too. And there was the driver. We wouldn't have had a chance. Besides, if he thinks we don't suspect, we may be able to get some valuable information later. I think -"

"What?"

"I'd better not say now. But remember this - we've got to look out for this driver. I think he'll take us straight to Ealing now. When we get to the barracks you stay in the cab - we'll pretend we may have to go back with him."

"I see," said Dick, thrilling with the excitement of this first taste of real war.

Harry was right. The driver's purpose in making such a long detour, whatever it was, had been accomplished. And now he plainly did his best to make up for lost time. He drove fast and well, and in a comparatively short time both the scouts could see that they were on the right track.

"You watch one side. I'll take the other," said Harry. "We've got to be able to find our way back to that house."

This watchfulness confirmed Harry's suspicions concerning the driver, because he made two or three circuits that could have no other purpose than to make it hard to follow his course.

At Ealing he and Dick carried out their plan exactly. Dick stayed with the cab, outside the wall; Harry hurried in. And five minutes after Harry had gone inside a file of soldiers, coming around from another gate, surrounded the cab and arrested the driver.

CHAPTER V

ON THE TRAIL

Harry had reached Colonel Throckmorton without difficulty and before delivering Major French's message, he explained his suspicions regarding the driver.

"What's that? 'Eh, what's that?" asked the colonel. "Spy? This country's suffering from an epidemic of spy fever - that's what! Still - a taxi cab driver, eh? Perhaps he's one of the many who's tried to overcharge me. I'll put him in the guardhouse, anyway! I'll find out if you're right later, young man!"

As a matter of fact, and as Harry surmised, Colonel Throckmorton felt that it was not a time to take chances. He was almost sure that Harry was letting his imagination run away with him, but it would be safer to arrest a man by mistake than to let him go if there was a chance that he was guilty. So he gave the order and then turned to question Harry. The scout first gave Major French's message, and Colonel Throckmorton immediately dispatched an orderly after giving him certain whispered instructions.

"Now tell me just why you suspect your driver. Explain exactly what happened," he said. He turned to a stenographer. "Take notes of this, Johnson," he directed.

Harry told his story simply and well. When he quoted the officer's remark to the cab driver, with the German inversion, the colonel chuckled.

"You have your way lost!' Eh ?" he said, with a smile. "You're right - he was no Englishman! Go on!"

When he had finished, the colonel brought down his fist on his desk with a great blow.

"You've done very well, Fleming - that's your name? - very well, indeed," he said, heartily. "We know London is covered with spies but we have flattered ourselves that it didn't matter very much what they found, since there was no way that we could see for them to get their news to their headquarters in Germany. But now -"

He frowned thoughtfully.

"They might be able to set up a. chain of signalling stations," he said. "The thing to do would be to follow them, eh? Do you think you could do that? You might use a motorcycle - know how to ride one?"

"Yes, sir," said Harry.

"Live with your parents, do you? Would they let you go? I don't think it would be very dangerous, and you would excite less suspicion than a man. See if they will let you turn yourself over to me for a few days. Pick out another scout to go with you, if you like. Perhaps two of you would be better than one. Report to me in the morning. I'll write a note to your scoutmaster - Mr. Wharton, isn't it? Right!"

As they made their way homeward, thoroughly worked up by the excitement of their adventure, Harry wondered whether his father would let him undertake this service Colonel Throckmorton had suggested. After all, he was not English, and he felt that his father might not want him to do it, although Mr. Fleming, he knew, sympathized strongly with the English in the war. He said nothing to Dick, preferring to wait until he was sure that he could go ahead with his plans.

But when he reached his house he found that things had changed considerably in his absence. Both his parents seemed worried; his father seemed especially troubled.

"Harry," he said, "the war has hit us already. I'm called home by cable, and at the same time there is word that your Aunt Mary is seriously ill. Your mother wants to be with her. I find that, by a stroke of luck, I can get quarters for your mother and myself on tomorrow's steamer. But there's no room for you. Do you think you could get along all right if you were left here? I'll arrange for supplies for the house; Mrs. Grimshaw can keep house. And you will have what money you need."

"Of course I can get along!" said Harry, stoutly. "I suppose the steamers are fearfully crowded?"

"Only about half of them are now in service," said Mr. Fleming. "And the rush of Americans who have been travelling abroad is simply tremendous. Well, if you can manage, it will relieve us greatly. I think we'll be back in less than a month. Keep out of mischief. And write to us as often as you can hear of a steamer that is sailing. If anything happens to you, cable. I'll arrange with Mr. Bruce, at the Embassy, to help you if you need him, but that ought not to be necessary."

Harry was genuinely sorry for his mother's distress at leaving him, but he was also relieved, in a way. He felt now he would not be forbidden to do his part with the scouts. He would be able to undertake what promised to be the greatest adventure that had ever come his way. He had no fear of being left alone for his training as a Boy Scout had made him too self reliant for that.

Mr. and Mrs. Fleming started for Liverpool that night. Train service throughout the country was so disorganized by the military use of the railways that journeys that in normal, peaceful times required only two or three hours were likely to consume a full day. So he went into the city of London with them and saw them off at Euston, which was full of distressed American refugees.

The Flemings found many friends there, of whose very presence in London they were ignorant, and Mr. Fleming, who, thanks to his business connections in London, was plentifully supplied with cash, was able to relieve the distress of some of them.

Many had escaped from France, Germany and Austria with only the clothes they wore, having lost all their luggage. Many more, though possessed of letters of credit or travellers' checks for considerable sums, didn't have enough money to buy a sandwich; since the banks were all closed and no one would cash their checks.

So Harry had another glimpse of the effects of war, seeing how it affected a great many people who not only had nothing to do with the fighting, but were citizens of a neutral nation. He was beginning to understand very thoroughly by this time that war was not what he had always dreamed. It meant more than fighting, more than glory.

But, after all, now that war had come, it was no time to think of such things. He had undertaken, if he could get permission, to do a certain very important piece of work. And now, by a happy accident, as he regarded it, it wasn't necessary for him to ask that permission. He was not forbidden to do any particular thing; his father had simply warned him to be careful.

So when he went home, he whistled outside of Dick Mercer's window, woke him up, and, when Dick came down into the garden, explained to him what Colonel Throckmorton wanted them to do.

"He said I could pick out someone to go with me, Dick," Harry explained. "And, of course, I'd rather have you than anyone I can think of. Will you come along?"

"Will I!" said Dick. "What do you think you'll do, Harry?"

"We may get special orders, of course," said Harry. "But I think the first thing will be to find out just where the signals from that house are being received. They must be answered, you know, so we ought to find the next station. Then, from that, we can work on to the next."

"Where do you suppose those signals go to?"

"That's what we've got to find out, Dick! But I should think, in the long run, to someplace on the East coast. Perhaps they've got some way there of signalling to ships at sea. Anyhow, that's what's got to be discovered. Did you see Graves tonight ?"

"No," said Dick, his lips tightening, "I didn't! But I heard about him, all right."

"How? What do you mean?"

"I heard that he'd been doing a tot of talking about you. He said it wasn't fair to have taken you and given you the honor of doing something when there were English boys who were just as capable of doing it as you."

"Oh!" said Harry, with a laugh. "Much I care what he says!"

"Much I care, either!" echoed Dick. "But, Harry, he has made some of the other chaps feel that way, too. They all like you, and they don't like him. But they do seem to think some of them should have been chosen."

"'Well, it's not my fault," said Harry, cheerfully. "I certainly wasn't going to refuse. And it isn't as if I'd asked Mr. Wharton to pick me out."

"No, and I fancy there aren't many of them who would have done as well as you did today, either!"

"Oh. yes, they would! That wasn't anything. We'd better get to bed now. I think we ought to report just as early as we can in the morning. If we get away by seven o'clock, it won't be a bit too early."

"All right. I'll be ready. Good-night, Harry!"

"Good-night, Dick!"

Morning saw them up on time, and off to Ealing. There Colonel Throckmorton gave them their orders.

"I've requisitioned motorcycles for you," he said. "Make sure of the location of the house, so that you can mark it on an ordnance map for me. Then use your own judgment, but find the next house. I have had letters prepared for you that will introduce you to either the mayor or the military commander in any town you reach and you will get quarters for the night, if you need them. Where do you think your search will lead you, Fleming?"

He eyed Harry sharply as he asked the question. "Somewhere on the East coast, I think, sir," replied Harry.

"Well, that remains to be seen. Report by telegraph, using this code. It's a simplified version of the official code, but it contains all you will need to use. That is all."

Finding the house, when they started on their motorcycles, did not prove as difficult a task as Harry had feared it might. They both remembered a number of places they had marked from the cab windows, and it was not long before they were sure they were drawing near.

"I remember that hill," said Harry. "By Jove - yes, there it is! On top of that hill, do you see? We won't go much nearer. I don't want them to see us, by any chance. All we need is to notice which way they're signalling."

They watched the house for some time before there was any sign of life. And then it was only the flashes that they saw. Since the previous day some sort of cover had been provided for the man who did the signalling.

"What do you make of it, Dick ?" asked Harry eagerly, after the flashing had continued for some moments.

"It looks to me as if they were flashing toward the north and a little toward the west," said Dick, puzzled.

"That's the way it seems to me, too," agreed Harry. "That isn't what we expected, either, is it?"

"Of course we can't be sure."

"No, put it certainly looks that way. Well, we can't make sure from here, but we've got to do it somehow. I tell you what. We'll circle around and get northwest of the house. Then we ought to be able to tell a good deal better. And if we get far enough around, I don't believe they'll see us, or pay any attention to us if they do."

So they mounted their machines again, and in a few moments were speeding toward a new and better spot from which to spy on the house. But this, when they reached it, only confirmed their first guess. The signals were much more plainly visible here, and it was obvious now, as it had not been before, that the screen they had noticed had been erected as much to concentrate the flashes and make them more easily visible to a receiving station as to conceal the operator. So they turned and figured a straight line as well as they could from the spot where the flashes were made. Harry had a map with him, and on this he marked, as well as he could, the location of the house. Then he drew a line from it to the northwest.

"The next station must be on this line somewhere," he said. "We'll stick to it. There's a road, you see, that we can follow that's almost straight. And as soon as we come to a high building we ought to be able to see both flashes - the ones that are being sent from that house and the answering signals. Do you see?"

"Yes, that'll be fine!" said Dick. "Come on!"

"Not so fast!" said a harsh voice behind them.

They spun around, and there, grinning a little, but looking highly determined and dangerous, was the same man they had seen the day before, and who had questioned them when the tire of their taxicab blew out! But now he was not in uniform, but in a plain suit of clothes.

"So you are spying on my house, are you?" he said. "And you lied to me yesterday! No troops were sent to Croydon at all!"

"Well, you hadn't any business to ask us!" said Dick, pluckily. "If you hadn't asked us any questions, we'd have told you no lies."

"I think perhaps you know too much," said the spy, nodding his head, "You had better come with me. We will look after you in this house that interests you so greatly."

He made a movement forward. His hand dropped on Dick's shoulder. But as it did so Harry's feet left the ground. He aimed for the spy's legs, just below the knee, and brought him to the ground with a beautiful diving tackle - the sort he had learned in his American football days. It was the one attack of all others that the spy did not anticipate, if, indeed, he looked for any resistance at all. He wasn't a football player, so he didn't know how to let his body give and strike the ground limply. The result was that his head struck a piece of hard ground with abnormal violence, and he lay prone and very still.

George Durston

"Oh, that was ripping, Harry!" cried Dick. "But do you think you've killed him?"

"Killed him? No!" said Harry, with a laugh.

"He's tougher than that, Dick!"

But he looked ruefully at the spy.

"I wish I knew what to do with him," he said. "He'll come to in a little while. But -"

"We can get away while he's still out," said Dick, quickly. "He can't follow us and we can get such a start with our motorcycles."

"Yes, but he'll know their game is up," said Harry. "Don't you see, Dick? He'll tell them they're suspected - and that's all they'll need in the way of warning. When men are doing anything as desperate as the sort of work they're up to in that house, they take no more chances than they have to. They'd be off at once, and start up somewhere else. We only stumbled on this by mere accident - they might be able to work for weeks if they were warned."

"Oh, I never thought of that! What are we to do, then?'

"I wish I knew whether anyone saw us from the house or if they didn't - ! Well, we'll have to risk that. Dick, do you see that house over there? It's all boarded up - it must be empty."

"Yes, I see it." Dick caught Harry's idea at once this time, and began measuring with his eye the distance to the little house of which Harry had spoken. "It's all down hill - I think we could manage it all right."

"We'll try it, anyhow," said Harry. "But first we'd better tie up his hands and feet. He's too strong for the pair of us, I'm afraid, if he should come to."

Once that was done, they began to drag the spy toward the house. Half carrying, half pulling, they got him down the slope, and with a last great effort lifted him through a window, which, despoiled of glass, had been boarded up. They were as gentle as they could be, for the idea of hurting a helpless man, even though he was a spy, went against the grain. But -

"We can't be too particular," said Harry. "And he brought it on himself. I'm afraid he'll have worse than this to face later on."

They dumped him through the window, from which they had taken the boards. Then they made their own way inside, and Harry began to truss up the prisoner more scientifically. He understood the art of tying a man very well indeed, for one of the games of his old scout patrol had involved tying up one scout after another to see if they could free themselves. And when he had done, he stepped back with a smile of satisfaction.

"I don't believe he'll get himself free very soon," he said. "He'll be lucky if that knock on the head keeps him unconscious for a long time, because he'll wake up with a headache, and if he stays as he is he won't know how uncomfortable he is."

"Are we going to leave him like that, Harry?"

"We've got to, Dick. But he'll be all right, I am going to telephone to Colonel Throckmorton and tell him to send here for him, but to do so at night, and so that no one will notice. He won't starve or die of thirst. I can easily manage to describe this place so that whoever the colonel sends will find it. Come on!"

They went back to their cycles and rode on until they came to a place where they could telephone. Harry explained guardedly, and they went on.

CHAPTER VI

THE MYSTERY OF BRAY PARK

"I hope he'll be all right," said Dick.

"They'll find him, I'm sure," said Harry. "Even if they don't, he'll be all right for a few days, two or three, anyhow. A man can be very uncomfortable and miserable, and still not be in any danger. We don't need half as much food as we eat, really. I've heard that lots of times."

They were riding along the line that Harry had marked on his map, and, a mile or two ahead, there was visible an old-fashioned house, with a tower projecting from its centre. From this, Harry had decided, they should be able to get the view they required and so locate the second heliographing station.

"How far away do you think it ought to be, Harry?" asked Dick.

"It's very hard to tell, Dick. A first-class heliograph is visible for a very long way, if the conditions are right. That is, if the sun is out and the ground is level. In South Africa, for instance, or in Egypt, it would work for nearly a hundred miles, or maybe even more. But here I should think eight or ten miles would be the limit. And it's cloudy so often that it must be very uncertain."

"Why don't they use flags, then?"

"The way we do in the scouts? Well, I guess that's because the heliograph is so much more secret. You see, with the heliograph the flashes are centered. You've got to be almost on a direct line with them, or not more than fifty yards off the centre line, to see them at all, even a mile away. But anyone can see flags, and read messages, unless they're in code. And if these people are German spies, the code wouldn't help them. Having it discovered that they were sending messages at all would spoil their plans."

"I see. Of course, though. That's just what you said. It was really just by accident that we saw them flashing."

Then they came to the house where they expected to make their observation. It was occupied by an old gentleman, who came out to see what was wanted and stood behind the servant who opened the door. At the sight of their uniforms he drew himself up very straight and saluted. But, formal as he was, there was a smile in his eyes.

"Well, boys," he said, "what can I do for you? On His Majesty's service, I suppose?"

"Yes, sir," said Dick. "We'd like to go up in your tower room, if you don't mind."

"Scouting, eh?" said the old gentleman, mystified. "Do you expect to locate the enemy's cavalry from my tower room? Well, well - up with you. You can do no harm."

Dick was inclined to resent the old gentleman's failure to take them seriously, but Harry silenced his protest. As they went up the stairs he whispered: "It's better for him to think that. We don't want anyone to know what we're doing, you know - not yet."

So they reached the tower room, and, just as Harry had anticipated, got a wonderful view of the surrounding country. They found that the heliograph they had left behind was working feverishly and Harry took out a pencil and jotted down the symbols as they were flashed.

"It's in code, of course," he said, "but maybe we'll find someone who can decipher it - I know they have experts for that. It might come in handy to know what they were talking about."

"There's the other station answering!" said Dick, excitedly, after a moment. "Isn't it lucky that it's such a fine day, Harry? See, there it is, over there!"

"Let me have the glasses," said Harry, taking the binoculars from Dick. "Yes, you're right! They're on the top of a hill, just about where I thought we'd find them, too. Come on! We've got no time to waste. They're a good seven miles from here, and we've a lot more to do yet."

Below stairs the old gentleman tried to stop them.

He was very curious by this time, for he had been thinking about them and it had struck him that they were too much in earnest to simply be enjoying lark. But Harry and Dick, while they met his questions politely, refused to enlighten him.

"I'm sorry, sir," said Harry, when the old gentleman pressed him too hard. "But I really think we mustn't tell you why we're here. But if you would like to hear of it later, we'll be glad to come to see you and explain everything."

"Bless my soul!" said the old man. "When I was a boy we didn't think so much of ourselves, I can tell you! But then we didn't have any Boy Scouts, either!"

It was hard to tell from his manner whether that was intended for a compliment or not. But they waited no longer. In a trice they were on their motorcycles and off again. And when they drew near to the hilltop whence the signals had come, Harry stopped. For a moment he looked puzzled, then he smiled.

"I think I've got it!" he said. "They're clever enough to try to fool anyone who got on to their signalling. They would know what everyone would think - that they would be sending their messages to the East coast, because that is nearest to Germany. That's why they put their first station here. I'll bet they send the flashes zig-zagging all around, but that we'll find they all get east gradually. Now we'll circle around this one until we find out in what direction it is flashing, then we'll know what line we must follow. After that all we've got to do is to follow the line to some high hill or building, and we'll pick up the next station."

Their eyes were more accustomed to the work now, and they wasted very little time. This time, just as Harry had guessed, the flashes were being sent due east, and judging from the first case that the next station would be less than ten miles away, he decided to ride straight on for about that distance. He had a road map, and found that they could follow a straight line, except for one break. They did not go near the hilltop at all.

"I'd like to know what they're doing there," said Dick.

"So would I, but it's open country, and they're probably keeping a close lookout. They're really safer doing that in the open than on the roof of a house, out here in the country."

"Because they can hide the heliograph? It's portable, isn't it?"

"Yes. They could stow it away in a minute, if they were alarmed. I fancy we'll find them using hilltops now as much as they can."

"Harry, I've just thought of something. If they've planned so carefully as this, wouldn't they be likely to have country places, where they'd be less likely to be disturbed?"

"Yes, they would. You're right, Dick. Especially as we get further and further away from London. I suppose there must be plenty of places a German could buy or lease."

"And perhaps people wouldn't even know they were Germans, if they spoke good English, and didn't have an accent."

That suggestion of Dick's bore fruit. For the third station they found was evidently hidden away In a private park. It was in the outskirts of a little village, and Harry and Dick had no trouble at all in finding out all the villagers knew of the place. "'Twas taken a year ago by a rich American gentleman, with a sight of motor cars and foreign-looking servants," they were told. "Very high and mighty he is, too - does all his buying at the stores in Lunnon, and don't give local trade any of his patronage."

The two scouts exchanged glances. Their suspicions were confirmed in a way. But it was necessary to be sure; to be suspicious was not enough for them.

"We'll have to get inside," he said under his breath to Dick. But the villager heard, and laughed.

"Easy enough, if you're friends of his," he said. "If not – look out, master! He's got signs up warning off trespassers, and traps and spring guns all over the place. Wants to be very private, and that, he does."

"Thanks," said Harry. "Perhaps we'd better not pay him a visit, after all."

The village was a sleepy little place, one of the few spots Harry had seen to which the war fever had not penetrated. It was not on the line of the railway, and there was not even a telegraph station. By showing Colonel Throckmorton's letter, Harry and Dick could have obtained the right to search the property that they suspected. But that did not seem wise.

"I don't think the village constables here could help us much, Dick," said Harry. "They'd give everything away, and we probably wouldn't accomplish anything except to put them on their guard. I vote we wait until dark and try to find out what we can by ourselves. It's risky but even if they catch us, I don't think we need to be afraid of their doing anything."

"I'm with you," said Dick. "We'll do whatever you say."

They spent the rest of the afternoon scouting around the neighboring country on their motorcycles, studying the estate from the roads that surrounded it. Bray Park, it was called, and it had for centuries belonged to an old family, which, however, had been glad of the high rent it had been able to extract from the rich American who had taken the place.

What they saw was that the grounds seemed to be surrounded, near the wall, by heavy trees, which made it difficult to see much of what was within. But in one place there was a break, so that, looking across velvety green lawns, they could see a small part of an old and weatherbeaten grey house. It appeared to be on a rise, and to stand several stories above the ground, so that it might well be an ideal place for the establishment of a heliograph station.

But Harry's suspicions were beginning to take a new turn.

"I believe this is the biggest find we've made yet, Dick," he said. "I think we'll find that if we discover what is really going on here, we'll be at the end of our task - or very near it. It's just the place for a headquarters."

"I believe it is, Harry. And if they've been so particular to keep everything about it secret, it certainly seems that there must be something important to hide," suggested Harry, thinking deeply. "I think I'll write a letter to Colonel Throckmorton, Dick. I'll tell him about this place, and that we're trying to get in and find out what we can about it. Then, if anything happens to us, he'll know what we were doing, and he will have heard about this place, even if they catch us. I'll post it before we go in."

"That's a splendid idea, Harry. I don't see how you think of everything the way you do."

"I think it's because my father's always talking about how one ought to think of all the things that can go wrong. He says that's the way he's got along in business is by never being surprised by having something unfortunate happen, and by always trying to be ready to make it as trifling as it can be."

So Harry wrote and posted his letter, taking care to word it so that it would be hard for anyone except Colonel Throckmorton to understand it. And, even after having purposely made the wording rather obscure, he put it into code. And, after that, he thought of still another precaution that might be wise. "We won't need the credentials we've got in there tonight, Dick," he said. "Nor our copies of the code, either. We'll bury them near where we leave our motorcycles. Then when we get out we can easily get them back, and if we should be caught they won't be found on us. Remember, if we are caught, we're just boys out trespassing. Let them think we're poachers, if they like."

But even Harry could think of no more precautions after that, and they had a long and tiresome wait until they thought it was dark enough to venture within the walls.

Getting over the wall was not difficult. They had thought they might find broken glass on top, but there was nothing of the sort. Once inside, however, they speedily discovered why that precaution was not taken - and also that they had had a remarkably narrow escape. For scarcely had they dropped to the ground and taken shelter when they saw a figure, carrying a gun, approaching. It was a man making the rounds of the wall. While they watched he met another man, also armed, and turned to retrace this steps.

"They've got two men, at least - maybe a lot more, doing that," whispered Harry. "We've got to find out just how often he passes that spot. We want to know if the intervals are regular, too, so that we can calculate just when he'll be there."

Three times the man came and went, while they waited, timing him. And Harry found that he passed the spot at which they had entered every fifteen minutes. That was not exact for there was a variation of a minute or so, but it seemed pretty certain that he would pass between thirteen and seventeen minutes after the hour, and so on.

"So we'll know when it's safe to make a dash to get out," said Harry. "The first thing a general does, you know, is to secure his retreat. He doesn't expect to be beaten, but he wants to know what he can live to fight another day if he is."

"We've got to retreat, haven't we?" asked Dick. "It wouldn't do us any good to stay here."

"That's so. But we've got to advance first. Now to get near that house, and see what we can find Look out for those traps and things our friend warned us of. It looks like just the place for them. And keep to cover!"

They wormed their way forward, often crawling along. Both knew a good deal about traps and how they are set, and their common sense enabled them to see the most likely places for them. They kept to open ground, avoiding shrubbery and what looked like windfalls of branches. Before they came into full view of the house they had about a quarter of a mile to go. And it was an exciting journey.

They dared not speak to one another. For all about, though at first they could see nothing, there was the sense of impending danger. They felt that unseen eyes were watching, not for them, perhaps, but for anyone who might venture to intrude and pass the first line. Both of the scouts felt that they were tilting against a mighty force, that the organization that would perfect, in time of peace. Such a system of espionage in the heart of the country of a possible enemy, was of the most formidable sort.

They stopped, at last, at the edge of the clump of thick, old trees that seemed to surround the place. Here they faced the open lawn, and Harry realized that to try to cross it was too risky. They would gain nothing by being detected. They could find out as much here by keeping their eyes and ears open, he thought, as by going forward, when they were almost sure to be detected.

"We'll stay here," he whispered to Dick, cautiously. "Dick, look over there - to the left of the house. You see where there's a shadow by that central tower? Well, to the left of that. Do you see some wires dangling there? I'm not sure."

"I think there are," whispered Dick, after a moment in which he peered through the darkness. Dick had one unusual gift. He had almost a savage's ability to see in the dark, although in daylight his sight was by no means out of the ordinary.

"Look!" he said, again, suddenly. "Up on top of the tower! There is something going up there - it's outlined against that white cloud!"

Harry followed with his eyes and Dick was right. A long, thin pole was rising, even as they looked on. Figures showed on the roof of the tower. They were busy about the pole. It seemed to grow longer as they watched. Then, suddenly, the dangling wires they had first noticed were drawn taut, and they saw a cross-piece on the long pole. And then, with a sudden rush of memory, Harry understood.

"Oh! We have struck it!" he said. "I remember now - a portable, collapsible wireless installation! I've wondered how they could use wireless, knowing that someone would be sure to pick up the signals and that the plant would be run down. But they have those poles made in sections - they could hide the whole thing. It takes very little time to set them up. This is simply a bigger copy of what they use in the field. We've got to get out!"

He looked at his watch.

"Carefully, now," he said. "We've just about got time. That sentry must be just about passing the place where we got over the wall now. By the time we get there he'll be gone, and we can slip out. We've got everything we came for, not that we've seen that!"

They started on the return journey through the woods. More than ever there seemed to be danger about them. And suddenly it reached out and gripped them - gripped Harry, at least. As he took a step his foot sank through the ground, as it seemed. The next moment he had all he could do to suppress a cry of agony as a trap closed about his ankle, wrenching it, and throwing him down.

"Go on!" he said to Dick, suppressing his pain by a great effort.

"I won't leave you!" said Dick. "I -"

"Obey orders! Don't you see you've go to go? You've got to tell them about the wireless - and about where I am! Or else how am I go get away? Perhaps if you come back quickly with help they won't find me until you come! Hurry - hurry!"

Dick understood. And, with a groan, he obeyed orders, and went.

CHAPTER VII

A CLOSE SHAVE

Probably Dick did not realize that he was really showing a high order of courage in going while Harry remained behind, aught in that cruel trap and practically in the hands of enemies who were most unlikely to treat him well. In fact, as he made his way toward the wall, Dick was reproaching himself bitterly.

"I ought to stay!" he kept on saying to himself over and over again. "I ought not to leave him so! He made me go so that I would be safe!"

There had been no time to argue, or Harry might have been able to make him understand that it was at least as dangerous to go as to stay - perhaps even more dangerous. Dick did not think that there was at least a chance that every trap was wired, so that springing it would sound an alarm in some central spot. If that were so, as Harry had fully understood, escape for Dick would be most difficult and probably he too would be captured.

"I'm such a coward!" Dick almost sobbed to himself, for he was frightened, though, it must be said, less on his account than at the thought of Harry. Yet he did not stop. He went on resolutely, alone, as he got used to the idea that he must depend on himself, without Harry to help him in any emergency that arose, his courage returned. He stopped, just as he knew Harry would have done, several feet short of the wall.

His watch told him that he had time enough to make a dash, had several minutes to spare, in fact. But he made sure.

And it was well that he did. For some alarm had been given. He heard footsteps of running men, and in a moment two men, neither of them the one they knew as the sentry, came running along the wall. They carried pocket flashlights, and were examining the ground carefully. Dick sensed at once what they meant to do, and shrank into the shelter of a great rhododendron bush. He was small for his age, and exceptionally lissome and he felt that the leaves would conceal him for a few moments at least. He was taking a risk of finding a trap in the bush, but it was the lesser of the two evils just then. And luck favored him. He encountered no trap.

Then one of the men with flashlights gave a cry that sounded to Dick just like the note of a dog that has picked up a lost scent. The lights were playing on the ground just where they had crossed the wall.

"Footsteps, Hans!" said the man. "Turned from the wall, too! They have gone in, but have not come out."

"How many?" asked the other man, coming up quickly.

"Two, I think - no more," said the discoverer. "Now we shall follow them."

Dick held his breath. If they could follow the footsteps - and there was no reason in the world j to hope that they could not! - they would be bound to pass within a foot or two of his hiding-place. And, as he realized, they would, when they were past him, find the marks of his feet returning. They would know then that he was between them and the wall. He realized what that would mean. Bravely he nerved himself to take the one desperate chance that remained to him. They were far too strong for him to have a chance to meet them on even terms, all he could hope for was an opportunity to make use of his light weight and his superior speed. He knew that he could move two feet, at least, to their one. And so he waited, crouching, until they went by. The light flashed by the bush, for some reason, it did not strike it directly. That gave him a respite. Fortunately they were looking for footprints, not for their makers.

The moment they were by, Dick took the chance of making a noise, and pushed through the bush, to reach the other side. And, just as the cry of the man who first had seen the footprints sounded again, he got through. At once, throwing off all attempt at silence, he started running, crouched low. He was only a dozen feet from the wall he leaped for a projection a few feet up. By a combination of good luck and skill he reached it with his hands.

A moment later he had swarmed over the wall and dropped to the other side just as a shot rang out behind. The bullet struck the wall, chipped fragments of stone flew all over him. But he was not hurt, and he ran as he had, never known he could run, keeping to the side of the road, where he was in a heavy shadow.

As soon as he could, he burst through a hedge on the side of the road opposite the wall, and ran on, sheltered by the hedge until, to his delight, he plunged headfirst into a stream of water. The fall knocked him out for a moment, but the cold water revived him and he did not mind the scraped knee and the hurt knuckles he owed to the sharp stones in the bed of the little brook. He changed his course at once, following the brook, since in that no telltale footprints would be left.

Behind him he heard the sound of pursuit for a little while, but he judged that the brook would save him. He could not be pursued very far. Even in this sleepy countryside he would find it easy to get help, and the Germans, as he was now sure they were, would have to give up the chase. All that had been essential had been for him to get a few hundred feet from the park, after that he was safe.

But, if he was safe, he was hopelessly lost. At least he would have been, had he been an ordinary boy, without the scout training. He was in unknown country and he had been chased away from all the landmarks he had. It was of the utmost importance that he should reach as soon as possible, and, especially, without passing too near Bray Park, the spot where the motorcycles and the papers and codes had been cached. And, when he finally came to a full stop, satisfied that he no longer had anything to fear from pursuit, he was completely in the dark as to where he was.

However, his training asserted itself. Although Harry had been in charge, Dick had not failed to notice everything about the place where they made their cache that would help to identify it. That was instinct with him by this time, after two years as a scout; it was second nature. And, though it had been light, he had pictured pretty accurately what the place would look like at night. He remembered for instance, that certain stars would be sure to fill the sky in a particular relation to the cache. And now he looked up and worked out his own position. To do that he had to reconstruct, with the utmost care, his movements since he had left the cache to the moment when he and Harry had entered Bray Park.

But the chase had confused him, naturally. He had doubled on his track more than once, trying to throw his pursuers off. But by remembering accurately the position of Bray Park in its relation to the cache, and by concentrating as earnestly as he could to remember as much as possible of the course of his flight, he arrived presently at a decision of how he must proceed to retrieve the motorcycles and the papers.

As soon as he had done so he hurried on, feverishly, taking a course that, while longer than necessary, was essential since he dared not go near Bray Park. He realized thoroughly how much depended on his promptness. It was essential that Colonel Throckmorton should learn of the wireless station, which was undoubtedly powerful enough to send its waves far out to sea, even if not to the German coast itself.

And there was Harry. The only chance of rescue for him lay in what Dick might do. That thought urged him on even more than the necessity of imparting what they had learned.

So, scouting as he went, least he encounter some prowling party from Bray Park silently looking for him, he went on hastily. He was almost as anxious to avoid the village as the spy headquarters, for he knew that in such places strangers might be regarded with suspicion even in times of peace. And, while the war fever had not seemed to be in evidence that afternoon, he knew that it might have broken out virulently in the interval. He had heard the stories of spy baiting in other parts of the country; how, in some localities, scores of absolutely innocent tourists had been arrested and searched. So he felt he must avoid his friends as well as his enemies until he had means of proving his identity.

Delaying as he was by his roundabout course, it took him nearly an hour to come to scenes that were familiar. But then he knew that he had found himself, with the aid of the stars. Familiar places that he had marked when they made the cache appeared, and soon he reached it. But it was empty; motorcycles and papers - all were gone!

CHAPTER VIII

A FRIEND IN NEED

"As long as I can't be at home, I'd rather be here than anywhere in the world I can think of!"

Was it little more than a week, thought Harry Fleming, since he had uttered those words so lightly? Was it just a week since Grenfel, his English scoutmaster, had bidden the boys of his troop goodbye? Was it just two days since father and mother had been so suddenly recalled to the States? Was it just that very morning that he and his good chum Dick Mercer had been detailed on this mission which had led to the discovery of the secret heliographs so busily sending messages to the enemy across the North Sea? Was it just a few hours since the two Scouts, hot on the trail, had cached papers and motorcycles and started the closer exploration of that mysterious estate outside the sleepy English village, leased, so the village gossip had it, by a rich American who eccentrically denied himself to all comers and zealously guarded the privacy of his grounds?

Was it just a few moments since he had urged, even commanded, Dick Mercer to leave him, caught in a trap set for just such trespassers as they? Had he urged his chum to leave him in his agony, for the ankle was badly wrenched, and seek safety in flight? The terrible pain in his ankle and the agonizing fear both for himself and his chum made moments seem like hours and the happenings of these same moments appear as an awful dream.

George Durston

He could hear, plainly enough, the advance of the two searchers who had scared Dick into hiding in the rhododendron bush, he could even see the gleam of their flashlights, and was able, therefore, to guess what they were doing. For the moment it seemed impossible to him that Dick should escape. He was sure of capture himself in a few minutes, and, as a matter of fact, there were things that made the prospect decidedly bearable. The pain in his ankle from the trap in which he had been caught was excruciating. It seemed to him that he must cry out, but he kept silence resolutely. As long as there was a chance that he might not fall into the hands of the spies who were searching the grounds, he meant to cling to it.

But the chance was a very slim one, as he knew. He could imagine, without difficulty, just about what the men with the flashlights would do, by reasoning out his own course. They would look for footprints. These would lead them to the spot where he and Dick had watched the raising of the wireless mast, and thence along the path they had taken to return to the wall and to safety. Thus they would come to him, and he would be found, literally like a rat in a trap.

And then, quite suddenly, came the diversion created by Dick's daring dash for escape, when he sped from the bush and climbed the wall, followed by the bullets that the searchers fired after him. Harry started, hurting his imprisoned ankle terribly by the wrench his sudden movement gave. Then he listened eagerly for the cry he dreaded yet expected to hear that would tell him that Dick had been hit. It did not come. Instead, he heard more men running, and then in a moment all within the wall was quiet, and he could hear the hue and cry dying away as they chased him along the road outside.

"Well, by Jove!" he said to himself, enthusiastically, "I believe Dick's fooled them. I didn't think he had it in him! That's bully for him! He ought to get a medal for that!"

It was some moments before he realized fully that he had gained a respite, temporally at least. Obviously the two men who had been searching with flashlights had followed Dick, there was at least a good chance that no one else knew about him. He had decided that there was some system of signal wires that rang an alarm when a trap was sprung. But it might be that these two men were the only ones who were supposed to follow up such an alarm.

He carried a flashlight himself and now he took the chance of playing it on his ankle, to see if there was any chance of escape. He hooded the light with his hand and looked carefully. But what he saw was not encouraging. The steel band looked most formidable. It was on the handcuff principle and any attempt to work his foot loose would only make the grip tighter and increase his suffering. His spirits fell at that. Then the only thing his brief immunity would do for him would be to keep him in pain a little longer. He would be caught anyhow, and he guessed that, if Dick got away, he would find his captors in a savage mood.

Even as he let the flashlight wink out, since it was dangerous to use it more than was necessary, he heard a cautious movement within a few feet. At first he thought it was an animal he had heard, so silent were its movements. But in a moment a hand touched his own. He started slightly, but kept quiet.

"Hush - I'm a friend," said a voice, almost at his elbow. "'I thought you were somewhere around here but I couldn't find you until you flashed your light. You're caught in a trap, aren't you?"

"Yes," said Dick. "Who are you?"

"That's what I want to know about you, first," said the other boy - for it was another boy, as Harry learned from his voice. Never had a sound been more welcome in his ears than that voice. "Tell me who you are and what you two were doing around here. I saw you this afternoon and tracked you. I tried to before, but I couldn't, on account of your motorcycles. Then I just happened to see you, when you were on foot. Are you Boy Scouts?"

"Yes," said Harry. "Are you?"

"Yes. That's why I followed - especially when I saw you coming in here. We've got a patrol in the village, but most of the scouts are at work in the fields."

Rapidly, and in a whisper, Harry explained a little, enough to make this new ally understand.

"You'd better get out, if you know how, and take word," said Harry. "I think my chum got away, but it would be better to be sure. And they'll be after me soon."

"If they give us two or three minutes we'll both get out," said the newcomer, confidently. "I know this place with my eyes shut. I used to play here before the old family moved away. I'm the vicar's son, in the village, and I always had the run of the park until these new people came. And I've been in here a few times since then, too."

"That's all right," said Harry. "But how am I going to get out of this trap?"

"Let me have your flashlight a moment," said the stranger.

Harry gave it to him, and the other scout bent over his ankle. Harry saw that he had a long slender piece of wire. He guessed that he was going to try to pick the lock. And in a minute or less Harry heard a welcome click that told him his new found friend - a friend in need, indeed, he was proving himself to be, had succeeded. His ankle was free.

He struggled to his feet, and there was a moment of exquisite pain as the blood rushed through his ankle and circulation was restored to his numbed foot. But he was able to stand, and, although limpingly, to walk. He had been fortunate, as a matter of fact, in that no bone had been crushed. That might well have happened with such a trap, or a ligament or tendon might have been wrenched or torn, in which case he would have found it just about impossible to move at all. As it was, however, he was able to get along, though he suffered considerable pain every time he put his foot to the ground.

It was no time, however, in which to think of discomforts so comparatively trifling as that. When he was outside he would be able, with the other scout's aid, to give his foot some attention, using the first aid outfit that he always carried, as every scout should do. But now the one thing to be done, to make good his escape.

Harry realized, as soon as he was free, that he was not by any means out of the woods. He was still decidedly in the enemy's country, and getting out of it promised to be a difficult and a perilous task. He was handicapped by his lack of knowledge of the place and what little he did know was discouraging. He had proof that human enemies were not the only ones he had to fear. And the only way he knew that offered a chance of getting out offered, as well, the prospect of encountering the men who had pursued Dick Mercer, returning. It was just as he made up his mind to this that the other scout spoke again.

"We can't get out the way you came in," he said. "Or, if we could, it's too risky. But there's another way. I've been in here since these people started putting their traps around, and I know where most of them are. Come on!"

Harry was glad to obey. He had no hankering for command. The thing to do was to get out as quickly as he could. And so he followed, though he had qualms when he saw that, instead of going toward the wall, they were heading straight in and toward the great grey house. They circled the woods that gave them the essential protection of darkness, and always they got further and further from the place where Dick and Harry had entered. Harry understood, of course, that there were other ways of getting out but it took a few words to make him realize the present situation as it actually was.

"There's a spot on the other side they don't really guard at all," said his companion. "It's where the river runs by the place. They think no one would come that way. And I don't believe they know anything at all about what I'm going to show you."

Soon Harry heard the water rustling. And then, to his surprise, his guide led him straight into a tangle of shrubbery. It was hard going for him, for his ankle pained him a good deal, but he managed it. And in a moment the other boy spoke, and, for the first time, in a natural voice. "I say, I'm glad we're here!" he said, heartily. "D'ye see?"

"It looks like a cave," said Harry.

"It is, but it's more than that, too. This place is no end old, you know. It was here when they fought the Wars of the Roses, I've heard. And come on - I'll show you something!"

He led the way on into the cave, which narrowed as they went. But Harry, pointing his flashlight ahead, saw that it was not going to stop.

"Oh! A secret passage! I understand now!" he exclaimed, finally.

"Isn't it jolly?" said the other. "Can't you imagine what fun we used to have here when we played about? You see, this may have been used to bring in food in time of siege. There used to be another spur of this tunnel that ran right into the house. But that was all let go to pot, for some reason. This is all that is left. But it's enough. It runs way down under the river - and in a jiffy we'll be out in the meadows on the other side. I say, what's your name?"

They hadn't had time to exchange the information each naturally craved about the other before. And now, as they realized it, they both laughed. Harry told his name.

"Mine's Jack Young," said the other scout. "I say, you don't talk like an Englishman?"

"I'm not," explained Harry. "I'm American. But I'm for England just now - and we were caught here trying to find out something about that place."

They came out into the open then, where the light of the stars enabled them to see one another. Jack nodded.

"I got an idea of what you were after - you two," he said. "The other one's English, isn't he?"

"Dick Mercer? Yes!" said Harry, astonished. "But how did you find out about us?"

"Stalked you," said Jack, happily. "Oh, I'm no end of a scout! I followed you as soon as I caught you without your bicycles."

"We must have been pretty stupid to let you do it, though," said Harry, a little crestfallen. "I'm glad we did, but suppose you'd been an enemy! A nice fix we'd have been in!"

"That's just what I thought about you," admitted Jack. "You see, everyone has sort of laughed at me down here because I said there might be German spies about. I've always been suspicious of the people who took Bray Park. They didn't act the way English people do. They didn't come to church, and when the pater - I told you he was the vicar here, didn't I? - went to call, they wouldn't let him in! Just sent word they were out. Fancy treating the vicar like that!" he concluded with spirit. Harry knew enough of the customs of the English countryside to understand that the new tenants of Bray Park could not have chosen a surer method of bringing down both dislike and suspicion upon themselves.

"That was a bit too thick, you know," Jack went on. "So when the war started, I decided I'd keep my eyes open, especially on any strangers who came around. So there you have it. I say! You'd better let me try to make that ankle easier. You're limping badly."

That was true, and Harry submitted gladly to such ministrations as Jack knew how to offer. Cold water helped considerably, it reduced the swelling. And then Jack skillfully improvised a brace, that, binding the ankle tightly, gave it a fair measure of support.

"Now try that," he said. "See if it doesn't feel better!"

"It certainly does!" said Harry. "You're quite a doctor, aren't you? Well now the next thing to do is to try to find where Dick is. I know where he went - to the place where we cached our cycles and our papers."

Like Dick, he was hopelessly at sea, for the moment, as to his whereabouts. And he had, more-over, to reckon with the turns and twists of the tunnel, which there had been no way of following in the utter darkness. But Jack Young, who, of course, could have found his way anywhere within five miles of them blindfolded, helped him, and they soon found that they were less than half a mile from the place.

"Can you come on with me, Jack?" asked Harry. He felt that in his rescuer he had found a new friend, and one whom he was going to like very well, indeed, and he wanted his company, if it was possible.

"Yes. No one knows I am out," said Jack, frankly. "The pater's like the rest of them here - he doesn't take the war seriously yet. When I said the other day that it might last long enough for me to be old enough to go, he laughed at me. I really hope it won't, but I wouldn't be surprised if id did, would you?"

"No, I wouldn't. It's too early to tell anything about it yet, really. But if the Germans fight the way they always have before, it's going to be a long war."

They talked as they went, and, though Harry's ankle was still painful, the increased speed the bandaging made possible more than made up for the time it had required. Harry was anxious about Dick, he wanted to rejoin him as soon as possible. And so it was not long before they came near to the place where the cycles had been cached.

"We'd better go slow. In case anyone else watched us this afternoon, we don't want to walk into a trap," said Harry. He was more upset than he had cared to admit by the discovery that he and Dick had been spied upon by Jack, excellent though it had been that it was so. For what Jack had done it was conceivable that someone else, too, might have accomplished.

"All right. You go ahead," said Jack. "I'll form a rear guard - d'ye see? Then you can't be surprised."

"That's a good idea," said Harry. "There, see that big tree, that blasted one over there? I marked that. The cache is in a straight line, almost, from that, where the ground dips a little. There's a clump of bushes."

"There's someone there, too," said Jack. "He's tugging at a cycle, as if he were trying to get ready to start it."

"That'll be Dick, then," said Harry, greatly relieved. "All right - I'll go ahead!"

He went on then, and soon he, too, saw Dick busy with the motorcycle.

"Won't he be glad to see me, though?" he thought. "Poor old Dick! I'll bet he's had a hard time."

Then he called, softly. And Dick turned. But - it was not Dick. It was Ernest Graves!

CHAPTER IX

AN UNEXPECTED BLOW!

For a moment it would have been hard to lay which of them was more completely staggered and amazed.

"What are you doing here?" Harry gasped, finally.

And then, all at once, it came over him that it did not matter what Ernest answered, that there could be no reasonable and good explanation for what he had caught Graves doing.

"You sneak!" he cried. "What are you doing here - spying on us?"

He sprang forward, and Graves, with a snarling cry of anger, lunged to meet him. Had he not been handicapped by his lame ankle, Harry might have given a good account of himself in a hand-to-hand fight with Graves, but, as it was, the older boy's superior weight gave him almost his own way. Before Jack, who was running up, could reach them, Graves threw Harry off. He stood looking down on him for just a second.

"That's what you get for interfering, young Fleming!" he said. "There's something precious queer about you, my American friend. I fancy you'll have to do some explaining about where you've been tonight." Harry was struggling to his feet. Now he saw the papers in Graves' hand. "You thief!" he cried. "Those papers belong to me! You've stolen them! Give them here!"

But Graves only laughed in his face.

"Come and get them!" he taunted. And, before either of the scouts could realize what he meant to do he had started one of the motorcycles, sprung to the saddle, and started. In a moment he was out of sight, around a bend in the road. Only the put-put of the motor, rapidly dying away, remained of him. But, even in that moment, the two he left behind him were busy. Jack sprang to the other motorcycle, and tried to start it, but in vain. Something was wrong; the motor refused to start.

"That's what he was doing when I saw him first," cried Harry, with a flash of inspiration. "I thought it was Dick, trying to start his motor - it was Graves trying to keep us from starting it! But he can't have done very much - I don't believe he had the time. We ought to be able to fix it pretty soon."

"It's two miles to the repair place!" said Jack, blankly.

"Not to this repair shop," said Harry, with a laugh. The need of prompt and efficient action pulled him together. He forgot his wonder at finding Graves, the pain of his ankle, everything but the instant need of being busy. He had to get that cycle going and be off in pursuit, that was all there was to it.

"Give me a steady light," he directed. "I think he's probably disconnected the wires of the magneto - that's what I'd do if I wanted to put a motor out of business in a hurry. And if that's all, there's no great harm done."

"I don't see how you know all that!" wondered Jack. "I can ride one of those things, but the best I can do is mend a puncture, if I should have one."

"Oh!" said Dick, "it's easy enough," working while he talked. "You see, the motor itself can't be hurt unless you take an axe to it, and break it all up. But to start you've got to have a spark - and you get that from electricity. So there are these little

George Durston

wires that make the connection. He didn't cut them, thank Heaven! He just disconnected them. If he'd cut them I might really have been up a tree because that's the sort of accident you wouldn't provide for in a repair kit."

"It isn't an accident at all," said Jack, literally.

"That's right," said Harry. "That's what I meant, too. Now let's see. I think that's all. Good thing we came up when we did or he'd have cut the tires to ribbons. And there are a lot of things I'd rather do than ride one of these machines on its rims - to say nothing of how long the wheels would last if one tried to go fast at all."

He tried the engine; it answered beautifully.

"Now is there a telephone in your father's house, Jack?"

"Sure there is. Why?" for Jack was plainly puzzled.

"So that I can call you up, of course! I'm going after Graves. Later I'll tell you who he is. I'm in luck, really. He took Dick's machine - and mine is a good ten miles an hour faster. I can race him and beat him but, of course, he couldn't know which was the fastest. Dick's is the best looking. I suppose that's why he picked it."

"But where is Dick?"

"That's what I'm coming to. They may have caught him but I hope not. I don't think they did, either. I think he'll come along here pretty soon. And, if he does, he'll have an awful surprise."

"I'll stay here and tell him -"

"You're a brick, Jack! It's just what I was going to ask you to do. I can't leave word for him any other way, and I don't know what he'd think if he came here and found the cycles and all gone. Then take him home with you, will you? And I'll ring you up just as soon as I can. Good-bye!"

And everything being settled as far as he could foresee it then, Harry went scooting off into the night on his machine. As he rode, with the wind whipping into his face and eyes, and the incessant roar of the engine in his ears, he knew he was starting what was likely to prove a wild-goose chase. Even if he caught Graves, he didn't know what he could do, except that he meant to get back the papers.

More and more, as he rode on, the mystery of Graves' behavior puzzled him, worried him. He knew that Graves had been sore and angry when he had not been chosen for the special duty detail. But that did not seem a sufficient reason for him to have acted as he had. He remembered, too, the one glimpse of Graves they had caught before, in a place where he did not seem to belong.

And then, making the mystery still deeper, and defying explanation, as it seemed to him, was the question of how Graves had known, first of all, where they were, and of how he had reached the place.

He had no motorcycle of his own or he would not have ridden away on Dick's machine. He could not have come by train. Harry's head swam with the problem that presented itself. And then, to make it worse, there was that remark Graves had made. He had said Harry would find it hard to explain where he had been. How did he know where they had been? Why should he think it would be hard for them to explain their actions?

"There isn't any answer," he said to himself.

"And, if there was, I'm a juggins to be trying to find it now. I'd better keep my mind on this old machine, or it will ditch me! I know what I've got to do, anyhow, even if I don't know why."

George Durston

Mile after mile he rode, getting the very best speed he could out of the machine. Somewhere ahead of him, he was sure, riding back toward London, was Graves. In this wild pursuit he was taking chances, of course. Graves might have turned off the road almost anywhere. But if he had done that, there was nothing to be done about it, that much was certain. He could only keep on with the pursuit, hoping that his quarry was following the straight road toward London. And, to be sure, there was every reason for him to hope just that. By this time it was very late. No one was abroad, the countryside was asleep. Once or twice he did find someone in the streets of a village as he swept through, then he stopped, and asked it a man on another motorcycle had passed ahead of him. Two or three times the yokel he questioned didn't know, twice, however, he did get a definite assurance that Graves was ahead of him.

Somehow he never thought of the outrageously illegal speed he was making. He knew the importance of his errand, and that, moreover, he was a menace to nothing but the sleep of those he disturbed. No one was abroad to get in his way, and he forgot utterly that there might be need for caution, until, as he went through a fair sized town, he suddenly saw three policemen, two of whom were also mounted on motorcycles, waiting for him.

They waved their arms, crying out to him to stop, and, seeing that he was trapped, he did stop.

"Let me by," he cried, angrily. "I'm on government service!"

"Another of them?" One of the policemen looked doubtfully at the rest. "Too many of you telling that tale tonight. And the last one said there was a scorcher behind him. Have you got any papers? He had them!"

Harry groaned! So Graves had managed to strike at him, even when he was miles away. Evidently he, too, had been held up, evidently, also, he had used Harry's credentials to get out of the scrape speeding had put him in.

"No, I haven't any credentials," he said, angrily. "But you can see my uniform, can't you? I'm a Boy Scout, and we're all under government orders now, like soldiers or sailors."

"That's too thin, my lad," said the policeman who seemed to be recognized as the leader. "Everyone, we've caught for speeding too fast since the war began has blamed it on the war. We'll have to take you along, my boy. They telephoned to us from places you passed - they said you were going so fast it was dangerous. And we saw you ourselves."

In vain Harry pleaded. Now that he knew that Graves had used his credentials from Colonel Throckmorton, he decided that it would be foolish to claim his own identity. Graves had assumed that, and he had had the practically conclusive advantage of striking the first blow. So Harry decided to submit to the inevitable with the best grace he could muster.

"All right," he said. "I'll go along with you, officer. But you'll be sorry before it's over!"

"Maybe, sir," said the policeman. "But orders is orders, sir, and I've got to obey them. Not that I likes running a young gentleman like yourself in. But -"

"Oh, I know you're only doing your duty, as you see it, officer," he said. "Can't be helped - but I'm sorry. It's likely to cause a lot of trouble."

So he surrendered. But, even while he was doing so, he was planning to escape from custody.

CHAPTER X

A GOOD WITNESS

Dick's surprise and concern when he found the cache empty and deserted, with papers and motorcycles alike gone, may be imagined. For a moment he thought he must be mistaken, that, after all, he had come to the wrong place. But a quick search of the ground with his flashlight showed him that he had come to the right spot. He could see the tracks made by the wheels of the machine; he could see, also, evidences of the brief struggle between Harry and Graves. For a moment his mystification continued. But then, with a low laugh, Jack Young emerged from the cover in which he had been hiding.

"Hello, there!" he said. "I say, are you Dick Mercer?"

"Yes!" gasped Dick. "But however do you know? I never saw you before!"

"Well, you see me now," said Jack. "Harry Fleming told me to look for you here. He said you'd be along some time tonight, if you got away. And he was sure you could get away, too."

"Harry!" said Dick, dazed. "You've seen him? Where is he? Did he get away? And what happened to the cycles and the papers we hid there? Why -"

"Hold on! One question at a time," said Jack. "Keep your shirt on, and I'll tell you all I know about it. Then we can decide what is to be done next. I think I'll attach myself temporarily to your patrol."

"Oh, you're a scout, too, are you?" asked Dick.

That seemed to explain a good deal. He was used to having scouts turn up to help him out of trouble. And so he listened as patiently as he could, while Jack explained what had happened. "And that's all I know," said Jack, finally, when he had carried the tale to the point where Harry rode off on the repaired motorcycle in pursuit of Ernest Graves. "I should think you might really know more about it now than I do."

"Why, how could I? You saw it all!"

"Yes, that's true enough. But you know Harry and I were too busy to talk much after we found that motor was out of order. All I know is that when we got here we found someone I'd never seen before and never want to see again messing about with the cycles. We thought it must be you, of course - at least Harry did, and of course I supposed he ought to know."

"And then you found it was Ernest Graves?"

"Harry did. He took one look at him and then they started right in fighting. Harry seemed to be sure that was the thing to do. If I'd been in his place I'd have tried to arbitrate I think. This chap Graves was a lot bigger than he. He was carrying weight for age. You see, I don't know yet who Graves is, or why Harry wanted to start fighting him that way. I've been waiting patiently for you to come along, so that you could tell me."

"He's a sneak!" declared Dick, vehemently. "I suppose you know that Harry's an American, don't you?"

"Yes, but that's nothing against him."

"Of course it isn't! But this Graves is the biggest and oldest chap in our troop - he isn't in our patrol. And he thought that if any of us were going to be chosen for special service, he ought to have the first chance. So when they picked Harry and me, he began talking about Harry's being an American. He tried to act as if he thought it wasn't safe for anyone who wasn't English to be picked out!"

"It looks as if he had acted on that idea, too, doesn't it, then? It seems to me that he has followed you down here, just to get a chance to play some trick on you. He got those papers, you see. And I fancy you'll be blamed for losing them."

"How did he know we were here?" said Dick, suddenly. "That's what I'd like to know!"

"Yes, it would be a good thing to find that out," said Jack, thoughtfully. "Well, it will be hard to do. But we might find out how he got here. I know this village and the country all around here pretty well. And Gaffer Hodge will know, if anyone does. He's the most curious man in the world. Come on - we'll see what he has to say."

"Who is he?" asked Dick, as they began to walk briskly toward the village.

"You went through the village this afternoon, didn't you? Didn't you see a very old man with white hair and a stick beside him, sitting in a doorway next to the little shop by the Red Dog?"

"Yes."

"That's Gaffer Hodge. He's the oldest man in these parts. He can remember the Crimean War and - oh, everything! He must be over a hundred years old. And he watches everyone who comes in. If a stranger is in the village he's never happy until he knows all about him. He was awfully worried today about you and Harry, I heard," explained Jack.

Dick laughed heartily.

"Well, I do hope he can tell us something about Graves. The sneak! I certainly hope Harry catches up to him. Do you think he can?"

"Well, he might, if he was lucky. He said the cycle he was riding was faster than the other. But of course it would be very hard to tell just which to way to go. If Graves knew there was a chance that he might be followed he ought to be able to give anyone who was even a mile behind the slip."

"Of course it's at night and that makes it harder for Harry."

"Yes, I suppose it does. In the daytime Harry could find people to tell him which way Graves was going, couldn't he?"

"Yes. That's just what I meant."

"Oh, I say, won't Gaffer Hodge be in bed and asleep?"

"I don't think so. He doesn't seem to like to go to bed. He sits up very late, and talks to the men when they start to go home from the Red Dog. He likes to talk, you see. We'll soon know - that's one thing. We'll be there now in no time."

Sure enough, the old man was still up when they arrived. He was just saying goodnight, in a high, piping voice, to a little group of men who had evidently been having a nightcap in the inn next to his house. When he saw Jack he smiled. They were very good friends, and the old man had found the boy one of his best listeners. The Gaffer liked to live in the past, he was always delighted when anyone would let him tell his tales of the things he remembered.

"Good-evening, Gaffer," said Jack, respectfully. "This is my friend, Dick Mercer. He's a Boy Scout from London."

"Knew it! Knew it!" said Gaffer Hodge, with a senile chuckle.

"I said they was from Lunnon this afternoon when I seen them fust! Glad to meet you, young master."

Then Jack described Graves as well as he could from his brief sight of him, and Dick helped by what he remembered.

"Did you see him come into town this afternoon, Gaffer?" asked Jack.

"Let me think," said the old man. "Yes - I seen 'un. Came sneaking in, he did, this afternoon as ever was! Been up to the big house at Bray Park, he had. Came in an automobile, he did. Then he went back there. But he was in the post office when you and t'other young lad from Lunnon went by, maister," nodding his head as if well pleased. This was to Dick, and he and Jack stared at one another. Certainly their visit to Gaffer Hodge had paid them well.

"Are you sure of that, Gaffer?" asked Jack, quietly. "Sure that it was an automobile from Bray Park?"

"Sure as ever was!" said the old man, indignantly. Like all old people, he hated anyone to question him, resenting the idea that anyone could think he was mistaken. "Didn't I see the machine myself - a big grey one, with black stripes as ever was, like all their automobiles?"

"That's true - that's the way their cars are painted, and they have five or six of them," said Jack.

"Yes. And he come in the car from Lunnon before he went there - and then he come out here. He saw you and t'other young lad from Lunnon go by, maister, on your bicycles. He was watching you from the shop as ever was."

"Thank you, Gaffer," said Jack, gravely. "You've told us just what we wanted to know. I'll bring you some tobacco in the morning, if you like. My father's just got a new lot down from London."

"Thanks, thank'ee kindly," said the Gaffer, overjoyed at the prospect.

Then they said good-night to the old man, who, plainly delighted at the thought that he had been of some service to them, and at this proof of his sharpness, of which he was always boasting, rose and hobbled into his house.

"He's really a wonderful old man," said Dick.

"He certainly is," agreed Jack. "His memory seems to be as good as ever, and he's awfully active, too. He's got rheumatism, but he can see and hear as well as he ever could, my father says."

They walked on, each turning over in his mind what they had heard about Graves.

"That's how he knew we were here," said Dick finally. "I've been puzzling about that. I remember now seeing that car as we went by. But of course I didn't pay any particular attention to it, except that I saw a little American flag on it."

"Yes, they're supposed to be Americans, you know," said Jack. "And I suppose they carry the flag so that the car won't be taken for the army. The government has requisitioned almost all the cars in the country, you know."

"I'm almost afraid to think about this," said Dick, after a moment of silence. "Graves must know those people in that house, if he's riding about in their car. And they -"

He paused, and they looked at one another.

"I don't know what to do!" said Dick. "I wish there was some way to tell Harry about what we've found out," Jack started.

"I nearly forgot!" he said. "We'd better cut for my place. I told

Harry we'd be there if he needed a telephone, you know. Come on!"

CHAPTER XI

THE FIRST BLOW

To Harry, as he was taken off to the police station, it seemed the hardest sort of hard luck that his chase of Graves should be interrupted at such a critical time and just because he had been over-speeding. But he realized that he was helpless, and that he would only waste his breath if he tried to explain matters until he was brought before someone who was really in authority. Then, if he had any luck, he might be able to clear things up. But the men who arrested him were only doing their duty as they saw it, and they had no discretionary power at all.

When he reached the station he was disappointed to find that no one was on duty except a sleepy inspector, who was even less inclined to listen to reason than the constables. "Everyone who breaks the law has a good excuse, my lad," he said. "If we listened to all of them we might as well close up this place. You can tell your story to the magistrate in the morning. You'll be well treated tonight, and you're better off with us than running around the country - a lad of your age! If I were your father, I should see to it that you were in bed and asleep before this."

There was no arguing with such a man, especially when he was sleepy. So Harry submitted, very quietly, to being put into a cell. He was not treated like a common prisoner, that much he was grateful for. His cell was really a room, with windows that were not even barred. And he saw that he could be very comfortable indeed.

George Durston

"You'll be all right here," said one of the constables. "Don't worry, my lad. You'll be let off with a caution in the morning. Get to sleep now - it's late, and you'll be roused bright and early in the morning."

Harry smiled pleasantly, and thanked the man for his good advice. But he had no intention whatever of taking it. He did not even take off his clothes, though he did seize the welcome chance to us the washstand that was in the room. He had been through a good deal since his last chance to wash and clean up, and he was grimmy and dirty. He discovered, too, that he was ravenously hungry. Until that moment, he had been too active, too busy with brain and body, to notice his hunger.

However, there was nothing to be done for that now. He and Dick had not stopped for meals that day since breakfast, and they had eaten their emergency rations in the early afternoon. In the tool case on his impounded motorcycle, Harry knew there were condensed food tables - each the equivalent of certain things like eggs, and steaks and chops. And there were cakes of chocolate, too, the most nourishing of foods that were small in bulk. But the knowledge did him little good now. He didn't even know where the motorcycle had been stored for the night. It had been confiscated, of course; in the morning it would be returned to him.

But he didn't allow his thoughts to dwell long on the matter of food. It was vastly more important that he should get away. He had to get his news to Colonel Throckmorton. Perhaps Dick had done that. But he couldn't trust that chance. Aside from that, he wanted to know what had become of Dick. And, for the life of him, he didn't see how he was to get away.

"If they weren't awfully sure of me, they'd have locked me up a lot more carefully than this," he reflected. "And of course it would be hard. I could get out of here easily enough."

He had seen a drain pipe down which, he felt sure, he could climb.

"But suppose I did," he went on, talking to himself. "I've got an idea it would land me where I could be seen from the door - and I suppose that's open all night. And, then if I got away from here, every policeman in this town would know me. They'd pick me up if I tried to get out, even if I walked."

He looked out of the window. Not so far away he could see a faint glare in the sky. That was London. He was already in the suburban chain that ringed the great city. This place - he did not know its name, certainly - was quite a town in itself. And he was so close to London that there was no real open country. One town or borough ran right into the next. The houses would grow fewer, thinning out, but before the gap became real, the outskirts of the next borough would be reached.

Straight in front of him, looking over the house tops, he could see the gleam of water. It was a reservoir, he decided. Probably it constituted the water supply for a considerable section. And then, as he looked, he saw a flash - saw a great column of water rise in the air, and descend, like pictures of a cloudburst. A moment after the explosion, he heard a dull roar. And after the roar another sound. He saw the water fade out and disappear, and it was a moment before he realized what was happening. The reservoir had been blown up! And that meant more than the danger and the discomfort of an interrupted water supply. It meant an immediate catastrophe - the flooding of all the streets nearby. In England, as he knew, such reservoirs were higher than the surrounding country, as a rule. They were contained within high walls, and, after a rainy summer, such as this had been, would be full to overflowing. He was hammering at his door in a moment, and a sleepy policeman, aroused by the sudden alarm, flung it open as he passed on his way to the floor below.

Harry rushed down, and mingled, unnoticed, with the policemen who had been off duty, but summoned now to deal with this disaster. The inspector who had received him paid no attention to him at all.

"Out with you, men!" he cried. "There'll be trouble over this - no telling but what people may be drowned. Double quick, now!"

They rushed out, under command of a sergeant. The inspector stayed behind, and now he looked at Harry.

"Hullo!" he said. "How did you get out?"

"I want to help!" said Harry, inspired. "I haven't done anything really wrong, have I? Oughtn't I be allowed to do whatever I can, now that something like this has happened?"

"Go along with you!" said the inspector. "All right! But you'd better come back - because we've got your motorcycle, and we'll keep that until you come back for it."

But it made little difference to Harry that he was, so to speak, out on bail. The great thing was that he was free. He rushed out, but he didn't make for the scene of the disaster to the reservoir, caused, as he had guessed, by some spy. All the town was pouring out now, and the streets were full of people making for the place where the explosion had occurred. It was quite easy for Harry to slip through them and make for London. He did not try to get his cycle. But before he had gone very far he over took a motor lorry that had broken down. He pitched in and helped with the slight repairs it needed, and the driver invited him to ride along with him.

"Taking in provisions for the troops, I am," he said. "If you're going to Lunnon, you might as well ride along with me. Eh, Tommy?"

His question was addressed to a sleepy private, who was nodding on the seat beside die driver. He started now, and looked at Harry.

"All aboard!" he said, with a sleepy chuckle. "More the merrier, say I! Up all night - that's what I've been! Fine sort of war this is? Do I see any fightin'? I do not! I'm a bloomin' chaperone for cabbages and cauliflowers and turnips, bless their little hearts!"

Harry laughed. It was impossible not to do that.

But he knew that if the soldier wanted fighting, fighting he would get before long. Harry could guess that regular troops – and this man was a regular - would not be kept in England as soon as the territorials and volunteers in sufficient number had joined the colors. But meanwhile guards were necessary at home.

He told them, in exchange for the ride, of the explosion and the flood that had probably followed it.

"Bli'me!" said the soldier, surprised. "Think of that, now! What will they be up to next - those Germans? That's what I'd like to mow! Coming over here to England and doing things like that! I'd have the law on 'em - that's what I'd do!"

Harry laughed. So blind to the real side of war were men who, at any moment, might find themselves face to face with the enemy!

CHAPTER XII

THE SILENT WIRE

Probably Jack Young and Dick reached the vicarage just about the time that saw Harry getting into trouble with the police for speeding. The vicar was still up, he had a great habit of reading late. And he seemed considerably surprised to find that Jack was not upstairs in bed. At first he was inclined even to be angry, but he changed his mind when he saw Dick, and heard something of what had happened.

"Get your friend something to eat and I'll have them make a hot bath ready," said the vicar. "He looks as if he needed both!"

This was strictly true. Dick was as hungry and as grimy as Harry himself. If anything, he was in even worse shape, for his flight through the fields and the brook had enabled him to attach a good deal of the soil of England to himself. So the thick sandwiches and the bowl of milk that were speedily set before him were severely punished. And while he ate both he and Jack poured out their story. Mr. Young frowned as he listened. Although he was a clergyman and a lover of peace, he was none the less a patriot.

"Upon my word!" he said. "Wireless, you think, my boy?"

"I'm sure of it, sir," said Dick.

"And so'm I," chimed in Jack. "You know, sir, I've thought ever since war seemed certain that Bray Park would bear a lot of watching and that something ought to be done. Just because this is a little bit of a village, without even a railroad station, people think nothing could happen here. But if German spies wanted a headquarters, it's just the sort of place they would pick out."

"There's something in that," agreed the vicar, thoughtfully. But in his own mind he was still very doubtful. The whole thing seemed incredible to him. Yet, as a matter of fact, it was no more incredible than the war itself. What inclined him to be dubious, as much as anything else, was the fact that it was mere boys who had made the discovery.

He had read of outbreaks of spy fever in various parts of England, in which the most harmless and inoffensive people were arrested and held until they could give some good account of themselves. This made him hesitate, while precious time was being wasted.

"I hardly know what to do - what to suggest," he went on, musingly. "The situation is complicated, really. Supposing you are right, and that German spies really own Bray Park, and are using it as a central station for sending news that they glean out of England, what could be done about it?"

"The place ought to be searched at once every-one there ought to be arrested!" declared Jack, impulsively. His father smiled.

"Yes, but who's going to do it?" he said. "We've just one constable here in Bray. And if there are Germans there in any number, what could he do? I suppose we might send word to Harobridge and get some polite or some territorials over. Yes, that's the best thing to do."

But now Dick spoke up in great eagerness. "I don't know, sir," he suggested. "If the soldiers came, the men in the house there would find out they were coming, I'm afraid. Perhaps they'd get away, or else manage to hide everything that would prove the truth about them. I think it would be better to report direct to Colonel Throckmorton. He knows what we found out near London, sir, you see, and he'd be more ready to believe us."

"Yes, probably you're right. Ring him up, then. It's late, but he won't mind."

What a different story there would have been to tell had someone had that thought only half an hour earlier! But it is often so. The most trivial miscalculation, the most insignificant mistake, seemingly, may prove to be of the most vital importance. Dick went to the telephone. It was one of the old-fashioned sort, still in almost universal use in the rural parts of England, that require the use of a bell to call the central office. Dick turned the crank, then took down the receiver. At once he herd a confused buzzing sound that alarmed him.

"I'm afraid the line is out of order, sir," he said. And after fifteen minutes it was plain that he was right. The wire had either been cut or it had fallen or been short circuited in some other way. Dick and Jack looked at one another blankly. The same thought had come to each of them, and at the same moment.

"They've cut the wires!" said Dick. "Now what shall we do? We can't hear from Harry, either!"

"We might have guessed they'd do that!" said Jack. "They must have had some one out to watch us, Dick - perhaps they thought they'd have a chance to catch us. They know that we've found out something, you see! It's a good thing we stayed where we could make people hear us if we got into any trouble."

"Oh, nonsense!" said the vicar, suddenly. "You boys are letting your imaginations run away with you. Things like that don't happen in England. The wire is just out of order. It happens often enough, Jack, as you know very well!"

"Yes, sir," said Jack, doggedly. "But that's in winter, or after a heavy storm - not in fine weather like this. I never knew the wire to be out of order before when it was the way it is now."

"Well, there's nothing to be done, in any case," said the vicar. "Be off to bed, and wait until morning. There's nothing you can do now."

Dick looked as if he were about to make some protest, but a glance at Jack restrained him. Instead he got up, said good-night and followed Jack upstairs. There he took his bath, except that he substituted cold water for the hot, for he could guess what Jack meant to do. They were going out again, that was certain. And, while it is easy to take cold, especially when one is tired, after a hot bath, there is no such danger if the water is cold.

"Do you know where the telephone wire runs?" he asked Jack.

"Yes, I do," said Jack. "I watched the men when they ran the wire in. There are only three telephones in the village, except for the one at Bray Park, and that's a special, private wire. We have one here, Doctor Brunt has one, and there's another in the garage. They're all on one party line, too. We won't have any trouble in finding out if the wire was cut, I fancy."

Their chief difficulty lay in getting out of the house. True, Jack had not been positively ordered not to go out again, but he knew that if his father saw him, he would be ordered to stay in. And he had not the slightest intention of missing any part of the finest adventure he had ever had a chance to enjoy - not he! He was a typical English boy, full of the love of adventure and excitement for their own sake, even if he was the son of a clergyman. And now he showed Dick what they would have to do.

"I used to slip out this way, sometimes," he said. "That was before I was a scout. I - well, since I joined, I haven't done it. It didn't seem right. But this is different. Don't you think so, Dick?"

"I certainly do," said Dick. "Your pater doesn't understand, Jack. He thinks we've just found a mare's nest, I fancy."

Jack's route of escape was not a difficult one. It led to the roof of the scullery, at the back of the house, and then, by a short and easy drop of a few feet, to the back garden. Once they were in that, they had no trouble. They could not be heard or seen from the front of the house, and it was a simple matter of climbing fences until it was safe to circle back and strike the road in front again. Jack led the way until they came to the garage, which was at the end of the village, in the direction of London.

Their course also took them nearer to Bray Park, but at the time they did not think of this.

"There's where the wire starts from the garage, d'ye see!" said Jack, pointing. "You see how easily We can follow it - it runs along those poles, right beside the road."

"It seems to be all right here," said Dick.

"Oh, yes. They wouldn't have cut it so near the village," said Jack. "We'll have to follow it along for a bit, I fancy a mile or so, perhaps. Better not talk much, either. And, I say, hadn't we better stay in the shadow? They must have been watching us before - better not give them another chance, if we can help it," was Jack's very wise suggestion. They had traveled nearly a mile when Dick suddenly noticed that the telephone wire sagged between two posts, "I think it has been. Cut - and that we're near the place, too," he said then, "Look, Jack! There's probably a break not far from here,"

"Right, oh!" said Jack. "Now we must be careful. I've just thought, Dick, that they might have left someone to watch at the place where they cut the wire."

"Why, Jack?"

"Well, they might have thought we, or someone else, might come along to find out about it, just as we're doing. I'm beginning to think those beggars are mightily clever, and that if they think of doing anything, they're likely to think that we'll think of it. They've outwitted us at every point so far,"

So now, instead of staying under the hedge, but still in the road, they crept through a gap in the hedge, tearing their clothes as they did so, since it was a blackberry row, and went along still in sight of the poles and the wire, but protected by the hedge so that no one in the road could see them.

"There!" said Jack, at last. "See? You were right, Dick. There's the place - and the wire was cut, too! It wasn't an accident. But I was sure of that as soon as I found the line wasn't working."

Sure enough, the wires were dangling. And there was something else. Just as they stopped they heard the voices of two men.

"There's the break, Bill," said the first voice. "Bli'me, if she ain't cut, too! Now who did that? Bringing us out of our beds at this hour to look for trouble!"

"I'd like to lay my hands on them, that's all!" said the second voice. "A good job they didn't carry the wire away - 'twon't take us long to repair, and that's one precious good thing!"

"Linemen," said Jack. "But I wonder why they're here? They must have come a long way. I shouldn't be surprised if they'd ridden on bicycles. And I never heard of their sending to repair a wire at night before."

"Listen," said Dick. "Perhaps we will find out."

"Well, now that we've found it, we might as well repair it," said the first lineman, grumblingly. "All comes of someone trying to get a message through to Bray and making the manager believe it was a life and death matter!"

"Harry must have tried to telephone - that's why they've come," said Jack. "I was wondering how they found out about the break. You see, as a rule, no one would try to ring up anyone in Bray after seven o'clock or so. And of course, they couldn't tell we were trying to ring, with the wire cut like that."

"Oh, Jack!" said Dick, suddenly. 'If they're linemen, I believe they have an instrument with them. Probably we could call to London from here. Do you think they will let us do that ?"

"That's a good idea. We'll try it, anyway," said Jack. "Come on. It must be safe enough now. These chaps won't hurt us."

But Jack was premature in thinking that. For no sooner did the two linemen see them than they rushed for them, much to both lads' surprise.

"You're the ones who cut that wire," said the first, a dark, young fellow. "I've a mind to give you a good hiding!"

But they both rushed into explanations, and luckily, the other lineman recognized Jack.

"It's the vicar's son from Bray, Tom," he said. "Let him alone."

And then, while their attention was distracted, a bullet sang over their heads. And "Hands oop!" said in a guttural voice.

CHAPTER XIII

A TREACHEROUS DEED

Harry Fleming had, of course, given up all hope of catching Graves by a direct pursuit by the time he accepted the offer of a ride in the motor truck that was carrying vegetables for the troops in quarters in London. His only hope now was to get his information to Colonel Throckmorton as soon as possible. At the first considerable town they reached, where he found a telegraph office open, he wired to the colonel, using the code which he had memorized. The price of a couple of glasses of beer had induced the driver and the soldier to consent to a slight delay of the truck, and he tried also to ring up Jack Young's house and find out what had happened to Dick.

When he found that the line was out of order he leaped at once to the same conclusion that Jack and Dick had reached - that it had been cut on purpose. He could not stay to see if it would be repaired soon.

A stroke of luck came his way, however. In this place Boy Scouts were guarding the gas works and an electric light and power plant, and he found one squad just coming off duty. He explained something of his errand to the patrol leader, and got the assurance that the telephone people should be made to repair the break in the wire.

"We'll see to it that they find out what is the trouble, Fleming," said the patrol leader, whose name was Burridge.

"By the way, I know a scout in your troop - Graves. He was on a scout with us a few weeks ago, when he was visiting down here. Seemed to be no end of a good fellow."

Harry was surprised for he had heard nothing of this before. But then that was not strange. He and Graves were not on terms of intimacy, by any means. He decided quickly not to say anything against Graves. It could do no good and it might do harm.

"Right," he said. "I know him - yes. I'll be going, then. You'll give my message to Mercer or Young if there's any way of getting the line clear?"

"Yes, if I sit up until my next turn of duty," said Burridge, with a smile. "Good luck, Fleming."

Then Harry was off again. Dawn was very near now. The east, behind him, was already lighted up with streaks of glowing crimson. Dark clouds were massed there, and there was a feeling in the air that carried a foreboding of rain, strengthening the threat of the red sky. Harry was not sorry for that. There would be work at Bray Park that might well fare better were it done under leaden skies.

As he rode he puzzled long and hard over what he had learned. It seemed to him that these German spies were taking desperate chances for what promised to be, at best, a small reward. What information concerning the British plans could they get that would be worth all they were risking? The wireless at Bray Park, the central station near Willesden, whence the reports were heliographed - it was an amazingly complete chain. And Harry knew enough of modern warfare to feel that the information could be important only to an enemy within striking distance.

That was the point. It might be interesting to the Gennan staff to know the locations of British troops in England, and, more especially, their destinations if they were going abroad as part of an expeditionary force to France or Belgium. But the information would not be vital, it didn't seem to Harry that it was worth all the risk implied. But if, on the other hand, there was some plan for a German invasion of England, then he would have no difficulty in understanding it. Then knowledge of where to strike, of what points were guarded and what were not, would be invaluable.

"But what a juggins I am!" he said. "They can't invade England, even if they could spare the troops. Not while the British fleet controls the sea. They'd have to fly over."

And with that half laughing expression he got the clue he was looking for. Fly over! Why not? Flight was no longer a theory, a possibility of the future. It war, something definite, that had arrived. Even as he thought of the possibility he looked up and saw, not more than a mile away, two monoplanes of a well-known English army type flying low.

"I never thought of that!" he said to himself.

And now that the idea had come to him, he began to work out all sorts of possibilities. He thought of a hundred different things that might happen. He could see, all at once, the usefulness Bray Park might have. Why, the place was like a volcano! It might erupt at any minute, spreading ruin and destruction in all directions. It was a hostile fortress, set down in the midst of a country that, even though it was at war, could not believe that war might come borne to it.

He visualized, as the truck kept in its plodding way, the manner in which warfare might be directed from a center like Bray Park. Thence aeroplanes, skillfully fashioned to represent the British planes, and so escape quick detection, might set forth. They could carry a man or two, elude guards who thought the air lanes safe, and drop bombs here, there everywhere and anywhere. Perhaps some such aerial raid was responsible for the explosion that had freed him only a very few hours before. Warfare in England, carried on thus by a few men, would be none the less deadly because it would not involve fighting. There would be no pitched battles, that much he knew. Instead, there would be swift, stabbing raids. Water works, gas works, would be blown up. Attempts would be made to drop bombs in barracks, perhaps. Certainly every effort would be made to destroy the great warehouses in which food was stored. It was new, this sort of warfare, it defied the imagination. And yet it was the warfare that, once he thought of it, it seemed certain that the Germans would wage.

He gritted his teeth at the thought of it. Perhaps all was fair in love and war, as the old proverb said. But this seemed like sneaky, unfair fighting to him. There was nothing about it of the glory of warfare. He was learning for himself that modern warfare is an ugly thing. He was to learn, later, that it still held its possibilities of glory, and of heroism. Indeed, for that matter, he was willing to grant the heroism of the men who dared these things that seemed to him so horrible. They took their lives in their hands, knowing that if they were caught they would be hung as spies.

The truck was well into London now, and the dawn was full. A faint drizzle was beginning to fall and the streets were covered with a fine film of mud. People were about, and London was arousing itself to meet the new day. Harry knew that he was near his journey's end. Tired as he was, he was determined to make his report before he thought of sleep. And then, suddenly, around a bend, came a sight that brought Harry to his feet, scarcely able to believe his eyes. It was Graves, on a bicycle. At the sight of Harry on the truck he stopped. Then he turned.

"Here he is!" he cried. "That's the one!"

A squad of men on cycles, headed by a young officer, came after Graves.

"Stop!" called the officer to the driver.

Harry stared down, wondering.

"You there - you Boy Scout come down!" said the officer.

Harry obeyed, wondering still more. He saw the gleam of malignant triumph on the face of Graves. But not even the presence of the officer restrained him.

"Where are those papers you stole from me, you sneak ?" he cried.

"You keep away from me!" said Graves. "You Yankee!"

"Here, no quarreling!" said the officer. "Take him, men!"

Two of the soldiers closed in on Harry. He stared at them and then at the officer, stupefied.

"What - what's this?" he stammered.

"You're under arrest, my lad, on a charge of espionage!" said the officer. "Espionage, and conspiracy to give aid and comfort to the public enemy. Anything you say may be used against you."

For a moment such a rush of words came to Harry, that he was silent by the sheer inability to decide which to utter first. But then he got control of himself.

"Who makes this charge against me!" he asked, thickly, his face flushing scarlet in anger.

"You'll find that out in due time, my lad. Forward march!"

"But I've got important information! I must be allowed to see Colonel Throckmorton at once! Oh, you've got no idea how important it may be!"

"My orders are to place you under arrest. You can make

application to see anyone later. But now I have no discretion. Come! If you really want to see Colonel Throckmorton, you had better move on."

Harry knew as well as anyone the uselessness of appealing from such an order, but he was frantic. Realizing the importance of the news he carried, and beginning to glimpse vaguely the meaning of Graves and his activity, he was almost beside himself.

"Make Graves there give back the papers he took from me!" he cried.

"I did take some papers, lieutenant," said Graves, with engaging frankness. "But they were required to prove what I had suspected almost from the first - that he was a spy. He was leading an English scout from his own patrol into trouble, too. I suppose he thought he was more likely to escape suspicion if he was with an Englishman."

"It's not my affair," said the lieutenant, shrugging his shoulders. He turned to Harry. "Come along, my lad. I hope you can clear yourself. But I've only one thing to do - and that is to obey my orders."

Harry gave up, then, for the moment. He turned and began walking along, a soldier on each side. But as he did so Graves turned to the lieutenant.

"I'll go and get my breakfast, then, sir," he said. "I'll come on to Ealing later. Though, of course, they know all I can tell them already."

"All right," said the officer, indifferently.

"You're never going to let him go!" exclaimed Harry, aghast. "Don't you know he'll never come back?"

"All the better for you, if he doesn't," said the officer.

"That's enough of your lip, my lad. Keep a quiet tongue in your head. Remember you're a prisoner, and don't try giving orders to me."

CHAPTER XIV

THE TRAP

The bullet that sang over their heads effectually broke up the threatened trouble between Dick Mercer and Jack Young on one side, and the telephone linemen on the other. With one accord they obeyed that guttural order, "Hands oop!"

They had been so interested in one another and in the cut wire that none of them had noticed the practically noiseless approach of a great grey motor car, with all lights out, that had stolen up on them. But now, with a groan, Dick and Jack both knew it for one of the Bray Park cars. So, after all, Dick's flight had been in vain. He had escaped the guards of Bray Park once, only to walk straight into this new trap. And, worst of all, there would be no Jack Young outside to help this time, for Jack was a captive, too. Only - he was not!

At the thought Dick had turned, to discover that Jack was not beside him. It was very dark, but in a moment he caught the tiniest movement over the hedge, and saw a spot a little darker than the rest of the ground about it. Jack, he saw at once had taken the one faint chance there was, dropped down, and crawled away, trusting that their captures had not counted their party, and might not miss the boy.

Just in time he slipped through a hole in the hedge. The next moment one of the headlights in the grey motor flashed out, almost blinding the the rest of them, as they held up their hands. In its light from the car, four men, well armed with revolvers, were revealed.

"Donnerwetter!" said one. "I made sure there were four of them! So! Vell, it is enough. Into the car with them!"

No pretence about this chap! He was German, and didn't care who knew it. He was unlike the man who had disguised himself as an English officer, at the house of the heliograph, but had betrayed himself and set this whole train of adventure going by his single slip and fall from idiomatic English that Harry Fleming's sharp ears had caught.

Dick was thrilled, somehow, even while he was being roughly bundled toward the motor. If these fellows were as bold as this, cutting telephone wires, driving about without lights, giving up all secrecy and pretence, it must mean that the occasion for which they had come was nearly over. It must mean that their task, whatever it might be, was nearly accomplished - the blow they had come to strike was about ready to be driven home.

"'Ere, who are you a shovin' off?" complained one of the linemen, as he was pushed toward the motor. He made some effort to resist but the next moment he pitched forward. One of the Germans had struck him on the head with the butt of his revolver. It was a stunning blow, and the man was certainly silenced. Dick recoiled angrily from the sight, but he kept quiet. He knew he could do no good by interfering. But the sheer, unnecessary brutality of it shocked and angered him. He felt that Englishmen, or Americans, would not treat a prisoner so - especially one who had not been fighting. These men were not even soldiers, they were spies, which made the act the more outrageous. They were serving their country, however, for all that, and that softened Dick's feeling toward them a little. True, they were performing their service in a sneaky, underhanded way that went against his grain. But it was service, and he knew that England, too, probably used spies, forced to do so for self-defence. He realized the value of the spy's work, and the courage that work required. If these men were captured they would not share the fate of those surrendering in battle but would be shot, or hung, without ceremony.

A minute later he was forced into the tonneau of the car, where he lay curled up on the floor. Two of the Germans sat in the cushioned seat while the two linemen, the one who had been hit still unconscious, were pitched in beside him. The other two Germans were in front, and the car began to move at a snail's pace. The man beside the driver began speaking in German, his companion replied. But one of the two behind interrupted, sharply.

"Speak English, dummer kerl he exclaimed, angrily. "These English people have not much sense, but if a passerby should hear us speaking German, he would be suspicious. Our words he cannot hear and if they are in English he will think all is well."

"This is one of those we heard of this afternoon," said the driver. "This Boy Scout. The other is riding to London - but he will not go, so far."

He laughed at that, and Dick, knowing he was speaking of Harry, shuddered.

"Ja, that is all arranged," said the leader, with a chuckle. "Not for long that could not be. But we need only a few hours more. By this time tomorrow morning all will be done. He comes, Von Wedel?"

"We got the word tonight - yes," said the other man. "All is arranged for him. Ealing-Houndsditch, first. There are the soldiers. Then Buckingham Palace. Ah, what a lesson we shall teach these English! Then the buildings at Whitehall. We shall strike at the heart of their empire the heart and the brains!"

Dick listened, appalled. Did they think, then, that he, a boy, could not understand? Or were they so sure of success that it did not matter? As a matter of fact, he did not fully understand. Who was Von Wedel? What was he going to do when he came? And how was he coming?

However, it was not the time for speculation. There was the chance that any moment they might say something he would understand, and, moreover, if he got away, it was possible that he might repeat what he heard to those who would be able to make more use of it.

Just then the leader's foot touched Dick, and he drew away. The German looked down at him, and laughed. "Frightened!" he said. "We won't hurt you! What a country that sends its children out against us!"

His manner was kindly enough, and Dick felt himself warming a little to the big man in spite of himself.

"Listen, boy," said the leader. "You have seen things that were not for your eyes. So you are to be put where knowledge of them will do no harm - for a few hours. Then you can go. But until we have finished our work, you must be kept. You shall not be hurt - I say it."

Dick did not answer. He was thinking hard. He wondered if Jack would try to rescue him. They were getting very near Bray Park, he felt, and he thought that, once inside, neither Jack nor anyone else could get him out until these men who had captured him were willing. Then the car stopped suddenly. Dick saw that they were outside a little house.

"Get out," said the leader.

Dick and the telephone man who had not been hurt obeyed, the other lineman was lifted out, more considerately this time.

"Inside!" said the German with the thick, guttural voice. He pointed to the open door, and they went inside. One of the Germans followed them and stood in the open door.

"Werner, you are responsible for the prisoners. especially the boy," said the leader. "See that none of them escape. You will be relieved at the proper time. You understand?"

"Ja, Herr Ritter!" said the man. "Zu befehl!"

He saluted, and for the first time Dick had the feeling that this strange procedure was, in some sense, military, even though there were no uniforms. Then the door shut, and they were left in the house.

It was just outside of Bray Park - he remembered it now. A tiny box of a place it was, too, but solidly built of stone. It might have been used as a tool house. There was one window; that and the door were the only means of egress. The German looked hard at the window and laughed. Dick saw then that it was barred. To get out that way, even if he had the chance, would be impossible. And the guard evidently decided that. He lay down across the door.

"So!" he said. "I shall sleep - but with one ear open! You cannot get out except across me. And I am a light sleeper!"

Dick sat there, pondering wretchedly. The man who had been struck on the head was breathing stertorously. His companion soon dropped off to sleep, like the German, so that Dick was the only one awake. Through the window, presently, came the herald of the dawn, the slowly advancing light. And suddenly Dick saw a shadow against the light, looked up intently, and saw that is was Jack Young. Jack pointed. Dick, not quite understanding, moved to the point at which he pointed.

"Stay there!" said Jack, soundlessly. His lips formed the words but he did not utter them. He nodded up and down vehemently, however, and Dick understood him, and that he was to stay where he was. He nodded in return, and settled down in his new position. And then Jack dropped out of sight.

For a long time, while the dawn waxed and the light through

the window grew stronger, Dick sat there wondering. Only the breathing of the three men disturbed the quiet of the little hut. But then, from behind him, he grew conscious of a faint noise. Not quite a noise, either, it was more a vibration. He felt the earthen floor of the hut trembling beneath him. And then at last he understood.

He had nearly an hour to wait. But at last the earth cracked and yawned where he had been sitting. He heard a faint whisper.

"Dig it out a little - there's a big hole underneath. You can squirm your way through. I'm going to back out now."

Dick obeyed, and a moment later he was working his way down, head first, through the tunnel Jack had dug from the outside. He was small and slight and he got through, somehow, though he was short of breath and dirtier than he had ever been in his life when at last he was able to straighten up - free.

"Come on!" cried Jack. "We've got no time to lose. I've got a couple of bicycles here. We'd better run for it."

Run for it they did, but there was no alarm. Behind them was the hut, quiet and peaceful. And beyond the hut was the menace of Bray Park and the mysteries of which the Germans had spoken in the great grey motor car.

CHAPTER XV

A DARING RUSE

Harry, furious as he was when he saw Graves allowed to go off after false accusation that had caused his arrest, was still able to control himself sufficiently to think. He was beginning to see the whole plot now, or to think he saw it. He remembered things that had seemed trivial at the time of their occurrence, but that loomed up importantly now. And one of the first things he realized was that he was probably in no great danger, that the charge against him had not been made with the serious idea of securing his conviction, but simply to cause his detention for a little while, and to discredit any information he might have.

He could no longer doubt that Graves was in league with the spies on whose trail he and Dick had fallen. And he understood that, if he kept quiet, all would soon be all right for him. But if he did that, the plans of the Germans would succeed. He had already seen an example of what they could do, in the destruction of the water works. And it seemed to him that it would be a poor thing to fail in what he had undertaken simply to save himself. As soon as he reached that conclusion he knew what he must do, or, at all events, what he must try to do.

For the officer who had arrested him he felt a good deal of contempt. While it was true that orders had to be obeyed, there was no reason, Harry felt, why the lieutenant should not have shown some discretion. An officer of the regular army would have done so, he felt. But this man looked unintelligent and stupid. Harry felt that he might safely reply on his appearance. And he was right. The officer found himself in a quandary at once. His men were mounted on cycles; Harry was on foot. And Harry saw that he didn't quite know what to do.

Finally he cut the Gordian knot, as it seemed to him, by impounding a bicycle from a passing wheelman, who protested vigorously but in vain. All he got for his cycle was a scrap of paper, stating that it had been requisitioned for army use. And Harry was instructed to mount this machine and ride along between two of the territorial soldiers. He had been hoping for something like that, but had hardly dared to expect it. He had fully made up his mind now to take all the risks he would run by trying to escape. He could not get clear away, that much he knew. But now he, too, like Graves, needed a little time. He did not mind being recaptured in a short time if, in the meantime, he could be free to do what he wanted.

As to just how he would try to get away, he did not try to plan. He felt that somewhere along the route some chance would present itself, and that it would be better to trust to that than to make some plan. He was ordered to the front of the squad - so that a better eye could be kept upon him, as the lieutenant put it. Harry had irritated him by his attempts to cause a change in the disposition of Graves and himself, and the officer gave the impression now that he regarded Harry as a desperate criminal, already tried and convicted.

Harry counted upon the traffic, sure to increase as it grew later, to give him his chance. Something accidental, he knew, there must be, or he would not be able to get away. And it was not long before his chance came. As they crossed a wide street there was a sudden outburst of shouting. A runaway horse, dragging a delivery cart, came rushing down on the squad, and in a moment it was broken up and confused. Harry seized the chance. His bicycle, by a lucky chance, was a high geared machine and before anyone knew he had gone he had turned a corner. In a moment he threw himself off the machine, dragged it into a shop, ran out, and in a moment dashed into another shop, crowded with customers. And there for a moment, he stayed. There was a hue and cry outside. He saw uniformed men, on bicycles, dashing by. He even rushed to the door with the crowd in the shop to see what was amiss! And, when the chase had passed, he walked out, very calmly, though his heart was in his mouth, and quite unmolested got aboard a passing tram car.

He was counting on the stupidity and lack of imagination of the lieutenant, and his course was hardly as bold as it seemed. As a matter of fact it was his one chance to escape. He knew what the officer would think - that, being in flight, he would try to get away as quickly as possible from the scene of his escape. And so, by staying there, he was in the one place where on one would think of looking for him!

On the tram car he was fairly safe. It happened, fortunately, that he had plenty of money with him. And his first move, when he felt it was safe, was to get off the tram and look for a cab. He found a taxicab in a short time, one of those that had escaped requisition by the government, and in this he drove to an outfitting shop, were he bought new clothes. He reasoned that he would be looked for all over, and that if, instead of appearing as a Boy Scout in character dress of the organization, he was in ordinary clothes, he would have a better chance. He managed the change easily, and then felt that it was safe for him to try and get into communication with Dick.

In this attempt luck was with him again. He called for the number of the vicarage at Bray, only to find that the call was interrupted again at the nearest telephone center. But this time he was asked to wait, and in a minute he heard Jack Young's voice in his ear.

"We came over to explain about the wire's being cut," said Jack. "Dick's all right. He's here with me. Where are you?

We've got to see you just as soon as we can."

"In London, but I'm coming down. I'm going to try to get a motor car, too. I'm in a lot of trouble, Jack - it's Graves."

"Come on down. We'll walk out along the road towards London and meet you. We've got a lot to tell you, but I'm afraid to talk about it over the telephone."

"All right! I'll keep my eyes open for you."

Getting a motor car was not easy. A great many had been taken by the government. But Harry remembered that one was owned by a business friend of his father's, an American, and this, with some difficulty, he managed to borrow. He was known as a careful driver. He had learned to drive his father's car at home, and Mr. Armstrong knew it. And so, when Harry explained that it was a matter of the greatest urgency, he got it - since he had established a reputation for honor that made Mr. Armstrong understand that when Harry said a thing was urgent, urgent it must be.

Getting out of London was easy. If a search was being made for him - and he had no doubt that that was true - he found no evidence of it. His change of clothes was probably what saved him, for it altered his appearance greatly. So he came near to Bray, and finally met his two friends.

CHAPTER XVI

THE CIPHER

"What happened to you?" asked Jack and Dick in chorus.

Swiftly Harry explained. He told of his arrest as a spy and of his escape. And when he mentioned the part that Ernest Graves had played in the affair, Jack and Dick looked at one another.

"We were afraid of something like that, said Jack. "Harry, we've found out a lot of things, and we don't know what they mean! We're sure something dreadful is going to happen tonight. And we're sure, too, that Bray Park is going to be the centre of the trouble."

"Tell me what you know," said Harry, crisply. "Then we'll put two and two together. I say, Jack, we don't want to be seen, you know. Isn't there some side road that doesn't lead anywhere, where I can run in with the car while we talk?"

"Yes. There's a place about a quarter of a mile further on that will do splendidly," he replied.

"All right. Lead the way! Tell me when we come to it. I've just thought of something else I ought to never have forgotten. At least, I thought of it when I took the things out of my pockets while I was changing my clothes."

They soon came to the turning Jack had thought of, and a run of a few hundred yards took them entirely out of sight of the main road, and to a place where they were able to feel fairly sure of not being molested.

Then they exchanged stories. Harry told his first. Then he heard of Dick's escape, and of his meeting with Jack. He nodded at the story they had heard from Graffer Hodge.

"That accounts for how Graves knew," he said, with much satisfaction. "What happened then?"

When he heard of how they had thought too late of calling Colonel Throckmorton by telephone he sighed.

"If you'd only got that message through before Graves did his work!" he said. "He'd have had to believe you then, of course. How unlucky!"

"I know," said Jack. "We were frightfully sorry. And then we went out to find where the wire was cut, and then got Dick. But I got away, and I managed to stay fairly close to them. I followed them when they left Dick in a little stone house, as a prisoner, and I heard this - I heard them talking about getting a big supply of petrol. Now what on earth do they want petrol for? They said there would still be plenty left for the automobiles - and then that they wouldn't need the cars any more, anyhow! What on earth do you make of that, Harry?"

"Tell me the rest, then I'll tell you what I think," said Harry. "How did you get Dick out? And did you hear them saying anything that sounded as if it might be useful, Dick?"

"That was fine work!" he said, when he had heard a description of Dick's rescue. "Jack, you seem to be around every time one of us gets into trouble and needs help!"

Then Dick told of the things he had overheard - the mysterious references to Von Wedel and to things that were to be done to the barracks at Ealing and Houndsditch. Harry got out a pencil and paper then, and made a careful note of every name that Dick mentioned. Then he took a paper from his pocket.

"Remember this, Dick?" he asked. "It's the thing I spoke of that I forgot until I came across it in my pocket this morning."

"What is it, Harry?"

"Don't you remember what we watched them heliographing some messages, and put down the Morse signs? Here they are. Now the thing to do is to see if we can't work out the meaning of the code. If it's a code that uses words for phrases we've probably stuck, but I think its more likely to depend on inversions."

"What do you mean, Harry?" asked Jack. "I'm sorry I don't know anything about codes and ciphers."

"Why, there are two main sorts of codes, Jack, and, of course, thousands of variations of each of those principal kinds. In one kind the idea is to save words - in telegraphing or cabling. So the things that are likely to be said are represented by one word. For instance Coal, in a mining code, might mean 'struck vein at two hundred feet level.' In the other sort of code, the letters are changed. That is done in all sorts of ways, and there are various tricks. The way to get at nearly all of them is to find out which letter or number or symbol is used most often, and to remember that in an ordinary letter E will appear almost twice as often as any other letter - in English, that is."

"But won't this be in German?"

"Yes. That's just why I wanted those names Dick heard. They are likely to appear in any message that was sent. So, if we can find words that correspond in length to those, we may be able to work it out. Here goes, anyhow!"

For a long time Harry puzzled over the message. He transcribed the Morse symbols first into English letters and found they made a hopeless and confused jumble, as he had expected. The key to the letter E was useless, as he had also expected. But finally, by making himself think in German, he began to see a light ahead. And after an hour's hard work he gave a cry of exultation.

"I believe I've got it!" he cried. "Listen and see if this doesn't sound reasonable!"

"Go ahead!" said Jack and Dick, eagerly.

"Here it is," said Harry. "Petrol just arranged. Supply on way. Reach Bray Friday. Von Wedel may come. Red light markers arranged. Ealing Houndsditch Buckingham Admiralty War Office. Closing."

They stared at him, mystified.

"I suppose it does make sense," said Dick. "But what on earth does it mean, Harry?

"Oh, can't you see?" cried Harry. "Von Wedel is a commander of some sort - that's plain, isn't it? And he's to carry out a raid, destroying or attacking the places that are mentioned! How can he do that? He can't be a naval commander. He can't be going to lead troops, because we know they can't land. Then how can he get here? And why should he need petrol?"

They stared at him blankly. Then, suddenly, Dick understood.

"He'll come through the air!" he cried.

"Yes, in one of their big Zeppelins!" said Harry. "I suppose she has been cruising off the coast. She's served as a wireless relay station, too. The plant here at Bray Park could reach her, and she could relay the message on across the North Sea, to Helgoland or Wilhelmshaven. She's waited until everything was ready."

"That what they mean by the red light markers, then?"

"Yes. They could be on the roofs of houses, and masked, so that they wouldn't be seen except from overhead. They'd be in certain fixed positions, and the men on the Zeppelins would be able to calculate their aim, and drop their bombs so many degrees to the left or right of the red marking lights."

"But we've got aeroplanes flying about, haven't we?" said Jack. "Wouldn't they see those lights and wonder about them?"

"Yes, if they were showing all the time. But you can depend on it that these Germans have provided for all that. They will have arranged for the Zeppelin to be above the position, as near as they can guess them, at certain times - and the lights will only be shown at those times, and then only for a few seconds. Even if someone else sees them, you see, there won't be time to do anything."

"You must be right, Harry!" said Jack, nervously. "There's no other way to explain that message. How are we going to stop them?"

"I don't know yet, but we'll have to work out some way of doing it. It would be terrible for us to know what had been planned and still not be able to stop them! I wish I knew were Graves was. I'd like to..."

He stopped, thinking hard.

"What good would that do?"

"Oh, I don't want him - not just now. But I don't want him to see me just at present. I want to know where he is so that I can avoid him."

"Suppose I scout into Bray?" suggested Jack. "I can find out something that might be useful, perhaps. If any of them from Bray Park have come into the village today I'll hear about it."

"That's a good idea. Suppose you do that, Jack. I don't know just what I'll do yet. But if I go away from here before you come back, Dick will stay. I've got to think - there must be some way to beat them!"

George Durston

CHAPTER XVII

A CAPTURE FROM THE SKIES

Jack went off to see what he could discover, and Harry, left behind with Dick, racked his brains for some means of blocking the plan he was so sure the Germans had made. He was furious at Graves, who had discredited him with Colonel Throckmorton, as he believed. He minded the personal unpleasantness involved far less than the thought that his usefulness was blocked, for he felt that not information he might bring would be received now.

As he looked around it seemed incredible that such things as he was trying to prevent could even be imagined. After the early rain, the day had cleared up warm and lovely, and it was now the most perfect of things, a beautiful summer day in England. The little road they had taken was a sort of blind alley. It had brought them to a meadow, whence the hay had already been cut. At the far side of this ran a little brook, and all about them were trees. Except for the call of birds, and the ceaseless hum of insects, there was no sound to break the stillness. It was a scene of peaceful beauty that could not be surpassed anywhere in the world. And yet, only a few miles away, at the most, were men who were planning deliberately to bring death and destruction upon helpless enemies - to rain down death from the skies.

By very contrast to the idyllic peace of all about them, the terrors of war seemed more dreadful. That men who went to war should be killed and wounded, bat though it was, still seemed legitimate. But his driving home of an attack upon a city all unprepared, upon the many non-combatants who would be bound to suffer, was another and more dreadful thing. Harry could understand that it was war, that it was permissible to do what these Germans were planned. And yet -

His thoughts were interrupted by a sudden change in the quality of the noisy silence that the insects made. Just before he noticed it, half a dozen bees had been humming near him. Now he heard something that sounded like the humming of a far vaster bee. Suddenly it stopped, and, as it did, he looked up, his eyes as well as Dick's being drawn upward at the same moment. And they saw, high above them, an aeroplane with dun colored wings. Its engine had stopped and it was descending now in a beautiful series of volplaning curves.

"Out of essense - he's got to come down," said Harry, appraisingly, to Dick. "He'll manage it all right, too. He knows his business through and through, that chap."

"I wonder where he'll land," speculated Dick.

"He's got to pick an open space, of course," said Harry. "And there aren't so many of them around here. By Jove!"

"Look! He's certainly coming down fast!" exclaimed Dick.

"Yes - and, I say, I think he's heading for this meadow! Come on - start that motor, Dick!"

"Why? Don't you want him to see us?"

"I don't mind him seeing us - I don't want him to see the car," explained Harry. "We'll run it around that bend, out of sight from the meadow."

"Why shouldn't he see it?"

"Because if he's out of petrol, he'll want to take all we've got and we may not want him to have it. We don't know who he is, yet."

The car was moving as Harry explained. As soon as the meadow was out of sight, Harry stopped the engine and got out of the car.

"He may have seen it as he was coming down - the car, I mean," he said. "But I doubt it. He's got other things to watch. That meadow for one - and all his levers and his wheel. Guiding an aeroplane in a coast like that down the air is no easy job."

"Have you ever been up, Harry?"

"Yes, often. I've never driven one myself, but I believe I could if I had to. I've watched other people handle them so often that I know just about everything that has to be done.

"That's an English monoplane. I've seen them ever so often," said Dick. "It's an army machine, I mean. See it's number? It's just coming in sight of us now. Wouldn't you like to fly her though?"

"I'd like to know what it's doing around here," said Harry. "And it seems funny to me if an English army aviator has started out without enough petrol in his tank to see him through any flight he might be making. And wouldn't he have headed for one of his supply stations as soon as he found out he was running short, instead of coming down in country like this?"

Dick stared at him.

"Do you think it's another spy?" he asked.

"I don't think anything about it yet, Dick. But I'm not going to be caught napping. That's a Bleriot - and the British army flying corps uses Bleriots. But anyone with the money can buy one and make it look like an English army plane. Remember that."

There was no mistaking about the monoplane when it was once down. Its pilot was German; he was unmistakably so. He had been flying very high and when he landed he was still stiff from the cold.

"Petrol!" he cried eagerly, as he saw the two boys. "Where can I get petrol? Quick! Answer me!"

Harry shot a quick glance at Dick.

"Come on," he said, beneath his breath. "We've got to get him and tie him up."

The aviator, cramped and stiffened as he was by the intense cold that prevails in the high levels where he had been flying, was no match for them. As they sprang at him his face took on the most ludicrous appearance of utter surprise. Had he suspected that they would attack him he might have drawn a pistol. As it was, he was helpless before the two boys, both in the pink of condition and determined to capture him. He made a struggle, but in two minutes he was laying roped, tied, and utterly helpless. He was not silent; he breathed the most fearful threats as to what would happen to them. But neither boy paid any attention to him.

"We've got to get him to the car," said Harry. "Can we drag him?"

"Yes. But if we loosen his feet a little, he could walk," suggested Dick. "That would be ever so much easier for him, and for us too. I should hate to be dragged. Let's make him walk."

"Right - and a good idea!" said Harry. He loosened the ropes about the aviator's feet, and helped him to stand.

"March!" he said. "Don't try to get away - I've got a leading rope, you see."

He did have a loose end of rope, left over from a knot, and with this he proceeded to lead the enraged German to the automobile. It looked for all the world as if he were leading a dog, and for a moment Dick doubled up in helpless laughter. The whole episode had it's comic side, but it was serious, too.

"Now we've got to draw off the gasoline in the tank in this bucket," said Harry. The German had been bestowed in the tonneau, and made as comfortable as possible with rugs and cushions. His feet were securely tied again, and there was no chance for him to escape.

"What are you going to do?" asked Dick. "Are you going to try to fly in that machine?"

"I don't know, yet. But I'm going to have it ready, so that I can if I need to," said Harry. "That Bleriot maybe the saving of us yet, Dick. There's no telling what we shall have to do."

Even as he spoke, Harry was making new plans, rendered possible by this gift from the skies. He was beginning, at last, to see a way to circumvent the Germans. What he had in mind was risky, certainly, and might prove perilous in the extreme. But he did not let that aspect of the situation worry him. His one concern was to foil the terrible plan that the Germans had made, and he was willing to run any risk that would help him to do so.

"The Zeppelin is coming here to Bray Park - it's going to land here," said Harry. "And if it ever gets away from here there will be no way of stopping it from doing all the damage they have planned, or most of it. Thanks to Graves, we wouldn't be believed if we tell what we know - we'd probably just be put in the guard house. So we've got to try to stop it ourselves."

They had reached the Bleriot by that time. Harry filled the

tank, and looked at the motor. Then he sat in the driver's seat and practiced with the levers, until he decided that he understood them thoroughly. And, as he did this, he made his decision.

"I'm going into Bray Park tonight," he said. "This is the only way to get in."

"And I'm going with you," announced Dick.

CHAPTER XVIII

VINDICATION

At first Harry refused absolutely to consent to Dick's accompanying him, but after a long argument he was forced to yield.

"Why should you take all the risks when it isn't your own country, especially?" asked Dick, almost sobbing. "I've got a right to go! And, besides, you may need me."

That was true enough, as Harry realized. Moreover, he had been investigating the Bleriot, and he discovered that it was one of the new safety type, with a gyroscope device to insure stability. That day was almost without wind, and therefore it seemed that if such an excursion could ever be safe, this was the time. He consented in the end, and later he was to be thankful that he had.

Once the decision was taken, they waited impatiently for the return of Jack Young. Harry foresaw protests from Jack when he found out what they meant to do, but for him there as an easy answer - there was room in the aeroplane for only two people, and there was no way of carrying an extra passenger.

It was early dusk when Jack returned, and he had the forethought to bring a basket of food with him - cold chicken, bread and butter, and milk, as well as some fruit.

"I didn't find out very much," he said, "except this. Someone from London has been asking about you both. And this much more - at least a dozen people have come down to Bray Park today from London."

"Did you see any sign of soldiers from London?"

"No," said Jack.

He was disappointed when he found out what they meant to do, but he took his disappointment pluckily when he saw that there was no help for it. Harry explained very quietly to both Jack and Dick what he meant to do and they listened, open mouthed, with wonder.

"You'll have your part to play, Jack," said Harry. "Somehow I can't believe that the letter I wrote to Colonel Throckmorton last night won't have some effect. You have got to scout around in case anyone comes and tell them all I've told you. You understand thoroughly, do you?"

"Yes," said Jack, quietly. "When are you going to start?"

"There's no use going up much before eleven o'clock," said Harry. "Before that we'd be seen, and, besides, if a Zepplin is coming, it wouldn't be until after that. My plan is to scout to the east and try to pick her up and watch her descend. I think I know just about where she'll land - the only place where there's room enough for her. And then -"

He stopped, and the others nodded, grimly.

"I imagine she'll have about a hundred and twenty miles to travel in a straight line - perhaps a little less," said Harry. "She can make that in about two hours, or less. Big as they are, those airships are painted so that they're almost invisible from below. So if she comes by night, getting here won't be as hard a job as it seems at first thought."

Then the three of them went over in every detail the plan Harry had formed. Dick and Jack took their places in the monoplane and rehearsed every movement they would have to make.

"I can't think of anything else that we can provide for now," said Harry, at last. "Of course, we can't tell what will come up, and it would be wonderful if everything came out just as we have planned. But we've provided for everything we can think of. You know where you are to be, Jack?"

"Yes."

"Then you'd better start pretty soon. Good-bye, Jack!" He held out his hand. "We could never have worked this out without you. If we succeed you'll have a big part in what we've done."

A little later Jack said good-bye in earnest, and then there was nothing to do but wait. About them the voices of the insects and frogs changed, with the darkening night. The stars came out, but the night was a dark one. Harry looked at his watch from time to time and at last he got up.

"Time to start!" he said.

He felt a thrill of nervousness as the monoplane rose into the air. After all, there was a difference between being the pilot and sitting still in the car. But he managed very well, after a few anxious moments in the ascent. And once they were clear of the trees and climbing swiftly, in great spirals, there was a glorious sensation of freedom. Dick caught his breath at first, then he got used to the queer motion, and cried aloud in his delight.

Harry headed straight into the east when he felt that he was high enough. And suddenly he gave a cry.

"Look!" he shouted in Dick's ear. "We didn't start a moment

too soon. See her - that great big cigar-shaped thing, dropping over there?"

It was the Zepplin - the battleship of the air. She was dipping down, descending gracefully, over Bray Park.

"I was right!" cried Harry. "Now we can go to work at once - we won't have to land and wait!"

He rose still higher, then flew straight for Bray Park. They were high, but, far below, with lights moving about her, they could see the huge bulk of the airship, as long as a moderate sized ocean liner. She presented a perfect target.

"Now!" said Harry.

And at once Dick began dropping projectiles they had found in the aeroplane - sharply pointed shells of steel. Harry had examined these - he found they were really solid steel shot, cast like modern rifle bullets, and calculated to penetrate, even without explosive action, when dropped from a height.

From the first two that Dick dropped there was no result. But with the falling of the third a hissing sound came from below, and as Dick rapidly dropped three more, the noise increased. And they could see the lights flying - plainly the men were running from the monster. Its bulk lessened as the gas escaped from the great bag and then, in a moment more, there was a terrific explosion that rocked the monoplane violently. Had Harry not been ready for it, they might have been brought down.

But he had been prepared, and was flying away.

Down below there was now a great glare from the burning wreckage, lighting up the whole scene. And suddenly there was a sharp breaking out of rifle fire. At first he thought the men below had seen them, and were firing upward. But in a moment he saw the truth. Bray Park had been attacked from outside!

Even before they reached the ground, in the meadow where Harry and Jack had emerged from the tunnel, and Harry and Dick saw, to their wonder and delight, that the ground swarmed with khaki-clad soldiers. In the same moment Jack ran up to them.

"The soldiers have the place surrounded!" he cried, exultingly. "They must have believed your letter after all, Harry! Come on - there's a boat here! Aren't you coming over?"

They were rowing for the other shore before the words were well spoken. And, once over, they were seized at once by two soldiers.

"More of them," said one of the soldiers. "Where's the colonel?"

Without trying to explain, they let themselves be taken to where Colonel Throckmorton stood near the burning wreckage. At the sight of Harry his face lighted up.

"What do you know about this?" he asked, sternly, pointing to the wrecked airship.

Harry explained in a few words.

"Very good," said the colonel. "You are under arrest - you broke arrest this morning. I suppose you know that is a serious offense, whether your original arrest was justified or not?"

"I felt I had to do it, sir," said Harry. He had caught the glint of a smile in the colonel's eyes.

"Explain yourself, sir," said the colonel. "Report fully as to your movements today. Perhaps I shall recommend you for a metal instead of court marshalling you, after all."

And so the story came out, and Harry learned that the colonel had never believed Graves, but had chosen to let him think he did.

"The boy Graves is a German, and older than he seems," said the colonel. "He was here as a spy. He is in custody now, and you have broken up a dangerous raid and a still more dangerous system of espionage. If you hadn't come along with your aeroplane, we would never have stopped the raid. I had ordered aviators to be here, but it is plain that something has gone wrong. You have done more than well. I shall see to it that your services are properly recognized. And now be off with you, and get some sleep. You may report to me the day after tomorrow!"

Choose from Thousands of 1stWorldLibrary Classics By

Adolphus WilliamWard
Aesop
Agatha Christie
Alexander Aaronsohn
Alexander Kielland
Alexandre Dumas
Alfred Gatty
Alfred Ollivant
Alice Duer Miller
Alice Turner Curtis
Alice Dunbar
Ambrose Bierce
Amelia E. Barr
Andrew Lang
Andrew McFarland Davis
Anna Sewell
Annie Besant
Annie Hamilton Donnell
Annie Payson Call
Anton Chekhov
Arnold Bennett
Arthur Conan Doyle
Arthur Ransome
Atticus
B. M. Bower
Basil King
Bayard Taylor
Ben Macomber
Booth Tarkington
Bram Stoker
C. Collodi
C. E. Orr
C. M. Ingleby
Carolyn Wells
Catherine Parr Traill
Charles A. Eastman
Charles Dickens
Charles Dudley Warner
Charles Farrar Browne
Charles Ives
Charles Kingsley
Charles Lathrop Pack
Charles Whibley
Charles Willing Beale
Charlotte M. Braeme
Charlotte M.Yonge
Clair W. Hayes
Clarence Day Jr.
Clarence E. Mulford

Clemence Housman
Confucius
Cornelis DeWitt Wilcox
Cyril Burleigh
D. H. Lawrence
Daniel Defoe
David Garnett
Don Carlos Janes
Donald Keyholé
Dorothy Kilner
Dougan Clark
E. Nesbit
E.P.Roe
E. Phillips Oppenheim
Edgar Allan Poe
Edgar Rice Burroughs
Edith Wharton
Edward J. O'Biren
John Cournos
Edwin L. Arnold
Eleanor Atkins
Elizabeth Cleghorn
Gaskell
Elizabeth Von Arnim
Ellem Key
Emily Dickinson
Erasmus W. Jones
Ernie Howard Pie
Ethel Turner
Ethel Watts Mumford
Eugenie Foa
Eugene Wood
Evelyn Everett-Green
Everard Cotes
F. J. Cross
Federick Austin Ogg
Ferdinand Ossendowski
Francis Bacon
Francis Darwin
Frances Hodgson Burnett
Frank Gee Patchin
Frank Harris
Frank Jewett Mather
Frank L. Packard
Frederick Trevor Hill
Frederick Winslow Taylor
Friedrich Kerst
Friedrich Nietzsche
Fyodor Dostoyevsky

Gabrielle E. Jackson
Garrett P. Serviss
Gaston Leroux
George Ade
Geroge Bernard Shaw
George Ebers
George Eliot
George MacDonald
George Orwell
George Tucker
George W. Cable
George Wharton James
Gertrude Atherton
Grace E. King
Grant Allen
Guillermo A. Sherwell
Gulielma Zollinger
Gustav Flaubert
H. A. Cody
H. B. Irving
H. G. Wells
H. H. Munro
H. Irving Hancock
H. Rider Haggard
H. W. C. Davis
Hamilton Wright Mabie
Hans Christian Andersen
Harold Avery
Harold McGrath
Harriet Beecher Stowe
Harry Houidini
Helent Hunt Jackson
Helen Nicolay
Hendy David Thoreau
Henrik Ibsen
Henry Adams
Henry Ford
Henry Frost
Henry James
Henry Jones Ford
Henry Seton Merriman
Henry Wadsworth
Longfellow
Henry W Longfellow
Herbert A. Giles
Herbert N. Casson
Herman Hesse
Homer
Honore De Balzac

Horace Walpole
Horatio Alger, Jr.
Howard Pyle
Howard R. Garis
Hugh Lofting
Hugh Walpole
Humphry Ward
Ian Maclaren
Israel Abrahams
J.G.Austin
J. Henri Fabre
J. M. Barrie
J. Macdonald Oxley
J. S. Knowles
J. Storer Clouston
Jack London
Jacob Abbott
James Allen
James Lane Allen
James Andrews
James Baldwin
James DeMille
James Joyce
James Oliver Curwood
James Oppenheim
James Otis
Jane Austen
Jens Peter Jacobsen
Jerome K. Jerome
John Burroughs
John F. Kennedy
John Gay
John Glasworthy
John Habberton
John Joy Bell
John Milton
John Philip Sousa
Jonathan Swift
Joseph Carey
Joseph Conrad
Joseph Jacobs
Julian Hawthrone
Julies Vernes
Justin Huntly McCarthy
Kakuzo Okakura
Kenneth Grahame
Kate Langley Bosher
L. A. Abbot
L. T. Meade
L. Frank Baum
Laura Lee Hope

Laurence Housman
Leo Tolstoy
Leonid Andreyev
Lewis Carroll
Lilian Bell
Lloyd Osbourne
Louis Tracy
Louisa May Alcott
Lucy Fitch Perkins
Lucy Maud Montgomery
Lydia Miller Middleton
Lyndon Orr
M. H. Adams
Margaret E. Sangster
Margaret Vandercook
Maria Edgeworth
Maria Thompson Daviess
Mariano Azuela
Marion Polk Angellotti
Mark Overton
Mark Twain
Mary Austin
Mary Cole
Mary Rowlandson
Mary Wollstonecraft
Shelley
Max Beerbohm
Myra Kelly
Nathaniel Hawthrone
O. F. Walton
Oscar Wilde
Owen Johnson
P.G.Wodehouse
Paul and Mable Thorn
Paul G. Tomlinson
Paul Severing
Peter B. Kyne
Plato
R. Derby Holmes
R. L. Stevenson
Rabindranath Tagore
Rahul Alvares
Ralph Waldo Emmerson
Rene Descartes
Rex E. Beach
Richard Harding Davis
Richard Jefferies
Robert Barr
Robert Frost
Robert Gordon Anderson
Robert L. Drake

Robert Lansing
Robert Michael Ballantyne
Robert W. Chambers
Rosa Nouchette Carey
Ross Kay
Rudyard Kipling
Samuel B. Allison
Samuel Hopkins Adams
Sarah Bernhardt
Selma Lagerlof
Sherwood Anderson
Sigmund Freud
Standish O'Grady
Stanley Weyman
Stella Benson
Stephen Crane
Stewart Edward White
Stijn Streuvels
Swami Abhedananda
Swami Parmananda
T. S. Ackland
The Princess Der Ling
Thomas A. Janvier
Thomas A Kempis
Thomas Anderton
Thomas Bailey Aldrich
Thomas Bulfinch
Thomas De Quincey
Thomas H. Huxley
Thomas Hardy
Thomas More
Thornton W. Burgess
U. S. Grant
Valentine Williams
Victor Appleton
Virginia Woolf
Walter Scott
Washington Irving
Wilbur Lawton
Wilkie Collins
Willa Cather
Willard F. Baker
William Makepeace
Thackeray
William W. Walter
Winston Churchill
Yei Theodora Ozaki
Young E. Allison
Zane Grey

www.ingramcontent.com/pod-product-compliance
Lightning Source LLC
Chambersburg PA
CBHW051840170626
46807CB00003B/1275

* 9 7 8 1 4 2 1 8 1 5 3 2 9 *